Scorned

by

Josephine Templeton

To God – who has made so many miracles happen in my life that I cannot possibly count. Praise be to you in the highest!

*

To my best friend who also happens to be my husband – Mike. You always know how to make me laugh!

**THE CAST
OF
SCORNED
THE FALLEN ANGELLE SERIES
BOOK ONE**

Angels

    Fallen Angels
        Nate Godsonne, Satan
        Tabitha

    Celestial Angels
        Lecahel "Cal", a parole angel

    Kitchen Angel
        Vivian

Demons

    Shade Demon
        Robert

    The Nightlight Demons
        Bloody Mary
        Clown teacher
        Candyman teacher
        Monster teenagers

    Sangre Demon
        Lilith

Diabolus' everto canis

    Satan's demon dogs that hunt down fallen angels

Humans

Angelle Smythe, former fallen angel
Jackson Phillip Daniel, Arcane Hunter
Dusty, Arcane Hunter
Miss Mouse

Shapeshifter

Kate

Vampires

Ben St. Amant, bartender at The Lusty Crow Bar
Chadwick, Head of the Human Society (THS)
Marishka – 1st twin
Trina – 2nd twin
Audrey
The Liliam - daughters of Lilith; born vampires

Werewolf

Pete, bouncer at The Lusty Crow Bar

Weregator

Bob

Witch

Jeneen

*

From Angelle's Grimoire

† *The Human Society (THS)*
  ‡ *Supernatural society that devote their lives and souls to the protecting of innocents*

† *The Nightlight Kingdom*
  ‡ *Realm where Demon High School is located*

*

† *Angels*
  ‡ *Celestial*
    ~ *Have Celestial wings (made of feathers) which grants access to Gates of Heaven*
    ~ *Can read human minds*
    ~ *Cannot have children*

  ‡ *Fallen*
    ~ *Have black, leather wings*
    ~ *Allergic to silver*
    ~ *Recently fallen get dragged into Hell to have all the good "trained" out of them, which takes a few centuries*
    ~ *Can have children*
    ~ *When moving between realms, some of their ash/essence, gets left behind but quickly evaporates unless saved in a silver container*

† *Arcane Hunters*
  ‡ *Fanatical humans that hunt and kill the supernatural whether good or evil*

† *Blood Addict*
  ‡ *Human controlled by vampire with its blood*

† *Demons*
  ‡ *Shade Demon*
    ~ *Curses a human with a riddle, and if it goes unsolved, the demon consumes their soul. They live on but turn evil.*

  ‡ *Sangre Demon (Full Blooded)*
    ~ *Blood demon*
    ~ *Drinks human blood to stay in Earth's realm*
    ~ *When they mate with humans, their offspring are the born vampires*
    ~ *Can open portals at will with fire*
    ~ *Can control vampires*
    ~ *Can eat or drink*
    ~ *Can read minds*
    ~ *Can walk in sunlight*
    ~ *Do have reflections but run the risk of getting pulled into the mirror (or water) and remain trapped there. A black onyx worn around the neck keeps that from happening.*
    ~ *Eyes tint red when hungry or mad*

- ~ Able to touch holy symbols
- ~ Bodies explode into dust when destroyed
- ~ Weird darkness that flits through eyes
- ~ Methods of Destroying:
  - ≈ removal of fangs
  - ≈ decapitation
- ~ Physical Attributes in demon-mode
  - ≈ Body turns fire-engine red
  - ≈ Hair turns jet black
  - ≈ Hand enlarge with long black fingernails
  - ≈ Thick and curling horns that protrude from forehead
  - ≈ Voice deepens to a low baritone (both male and female)
  - ≈ 7 foot tall
  - ≈ Can throw fire bolts

‡ Sangre Demon (Half Full Blooded; Half Human)
- ~ Has all of the above except remain their same height
- ~ Mirrors steal their beauty or handsomeness
- ~ Males true forms resemble above
- ~ Females true forms resemble hags

- † *Vampires*
  - ‡ *Cannot eat or drink (including garlic, which makes them weak)*
  - ‡ *Cannot read minds*
  - ‡ *Cannot walk in sunlight unless on blood of a Werewolf*
  - ‡ *Allergic to Holy Water*
  - ‡ *Do not turn into bats*
  - ‡ *Do have reflections*
  - ‡ *Mirrors don't bother them*
  - ‡ *Eyes tint red when hungry or mad*
  - ‡ *Able to touch holy symbols*
  - ‡ *Bodies explode into dust when destroyed*
  - ‡ *Ancient ones*
    - ~ *Psychokinesis*
    - ~ *Cloaking ability*
  - ‡ *Two types*
    - ~ *Born Vampire*
      - ≈ *Created from a human and a Sangre Demon*
      - ≈ *Controlled by parent*
      - ≈ *Method of Destruction*
        - ⸰ *Death of parent*
        - ⸰ *Sunlight and staking puts them in a coma*
    - ~ *Sired Vampire*
      - ≈ *Humans that are bitten by a born vampire*
      - ≈ *Weaker than the Born*
      - ≈ *Controlled by sire but do not die if sire dies*
      - ≈ *Method of Destruction*
        - ⸰ *Staking the heart*
        - ⸰ *Sunlight*

The Lusty Crow

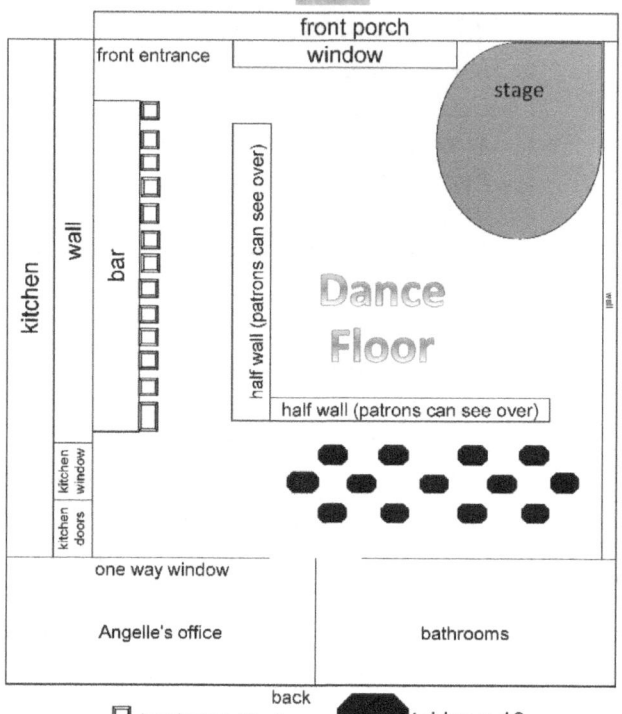

front porch

front entrance | window

stage

kitchen | wall | bar | half wall (patrons can see over)

Dance Floor

half wall (patrons can see over)

kitchen window | kitchen doors

one way window

Angelle's office | bathrooms

back door

barstools = 13   tables = 13

CHAPTER 1

I had been so naïve the day I fell from grace.

When I think of myself as a young angel, I cringe in disgust. I had followed love blindly, never truly understanding all the aspects it entailed. Through my rose-colored glasses, love's wings had been shiny and covered with valentine hearts and rainbows. I had never imagined the dark path love often traveled. Yet love survived and even flourished for others, but not for me.

***

Angelle's bathroom
Watson, Louisiana
Sunday, December 17th, 4:00 PM
Countdown: 14 Days 23 Hours 59 minutes 59 Seconds

I stepped into the dark bathroom and reached for the switch. Icy fingers wrapped around my left wrist, stopping me. I gasped as my heart jumped into my throat. I pressed my right hand to my chest, as if that would help calm the adrenaline pumping through me.

"Damn it, Robert."

"Well, I couldn't let you turn on the light to send me back to Hell yet, Angelle." His cold fingers slid away from my wrist.

My eyesight adjusted to the dark, and the demon came into focus. His short black hair stood up in disarray, and stubble covered his narrow chin. He smelled of sun, sand and ocean, and I wondered what demon chick had gotten him the cologne. I should send her a thank you card because I hated his normal smoky scent. Everyone has a special scent, and unfortunately, many beings stink worse than dog doo-doo.

"So how's the Shade demon business going these days?" I asked.

"Better than picking fleas off the hounds of Hell."

I shuddered. No fluffy puppies there. Hellhound creatures were all teeth. "Wise choice."

Before I could protest, Robert pressed his lips to mine. I was sweaty and grimy from my morning jog, and I wanted to push him away. *He couldn't have waited 'til I bathed?*

He pulled his head back. "Well? Did that kiss spark our old flame?"

I swiped at my lips with the back of my hand "It was ok, but no bells."

He slid his hands to my waist and kept me firmly in place. "I wish you hadn't become human. We could have spent eternity together."

I smiled as I recalled our bittersweet, whirlwind romance. "I love you, Robert, but I'm not *in love* with you. Get over me."

His hands relaxed their hold on me, and he stepped away with a deep chuckle. "Believe it or not, Angelle, I am. You're beautiful, but you aren't the only fallen angel in the sea."

"Jerk." I brushed past him and stepped in front of the mirror, pulling my long blonde hair out of the ponytail. After leaning in close to inspect the dark circles under my eyes, I turned on the water and waited for it to heat up. "I'm gonna get my wings back one day."

He moved to stand directly behind me. I watched his darkened figure in the mirror. "Fallen angels don't get their celestial wings back."

My heart twisted at the barb of his words. I lifted my nose in defiance. "Abbadona did."

Robert snorted. "That particular fallen angel dogged every step the archangel took. I hope you're not foolish enough to try that route."

"So you think Abbadona was a fool? Do you think I'm one for wanting to get back into Heaven?" I crossed my arms and tapped my foot. "I'll have you know, Robert Andrew de Bric the Third, the way into Heaven is *not* through the Archangel Michael."

"My point exactly," he whispered. I detected pity in his voice, which I abhorred. "Do you honestly think they'll let the leader of the lust demons in?"

Heat rose in my face as my heart ached and unwanted tears sprang to my eyes. I didn't want to remember the tortures I'd endured as the girlfriend of Satan (aka Nate) … nor the ones I had dished out. "I had no choice in the things I did. Satan made me do it."

"That's what they all say," Robert said.

I covered my face with a hot washcloth. No doubt about it. Memories can be painful. An image flashed in my head of Satan lashing a fellow fallen angel because I had refused to learn how to draw forth lust. He knew how to motivate me and often used my compassion for others against me.

When the silence became overwhelming, I slammed the rag into the sink before facing Robert. "Just give me the damn riddle."

The temperature dropped, and goose bumps rose on my bare arms. Robert's eyes glowed red, and his skin rippled as it changed from human-like to charcoal-colored scales. His inner demon scared the hell out of me. My fear was irrational because I knew he would never hurt me.

3

"Solve the riddle in fifteen days, and I won't eat your soul," Robert said in a demonic tone.

"Spare me the drama, Bob. I know the drill." My voice quivered, and I rolled my eyes, disgusted at myself. I had to take him off his demonic horse or my heart was going to burst from irrational fear.

"Gelle, don't call me that."

I ground my teeth at the nickname. I bit back a smart-ass retort because I wanted to get this done. As the temperature dropped another ten degrees, I shuddered from the chill.

"Ladies-in-waiting steal gentlemen's port to give to the bride who's forever scorned."

Robert slapped a thick gold bracelet around my left wrist. The riddle was inscribed on the bracelet. Thankfully, that part was on the same side as my palm. Beneath the black letters was a digital clock that slowly ticked down from 15 days. While the bracelet fit comfortably, I knew attempts to remove it would prove futile due to the magic infused into it. Upon answering the riddle and vanquishing the baddie associated with it, the bracelet would disappear.

I shook my head and sighed. I had always solved his riddles with ease. Hopefully this one would be just as easy.

The acrid scent of demon burned my nose as Robert finished his spell. He always smelled of ash when exerting his powers, and I would smell like Hell for days. Shampoo would take care of my hair, but I'd have to throw my clothes away.

"So glad you did this before I got a bath."

"I thought you'd like that." Robert's voice had returned to its hot silkiness. "But I dearly wanted to pop in on you while you were in the tub. I can hang around and keep you company if you'd like."

I ushered him toward the door. "See you later, Robert."

"I can wash your back."

"Goodbye, Robert." I stepped past him.

"Or even your hair."

I reached out and flicked on the light. "Adios, mi amigo."

"Oh, you're no fun, Ange-." His voice cut off as he slipped back into Hell's realm.

***

The Lusty Crow
Watson, LA
Sunday, December 17th, 6:00 PM
Countdown: 14 Days 21 Hours 59 minutes 59 Seconds

I shut the office door on the bar and dropped several daily newspapers on my desk. As was my routine, I grabbed a can of cranberry scented air freshener off the file cabinet and sprayed it before plopping into the desk chair. I didn't know which was worse…the perfume, cologne and beer fumes that lingered twenty-four seven or demon smoke.

I sighed, sat back, and scanned the bar through the one-way window. At 6 pm, the crowd was light, but that would pick up.

The Lusty Crow might not be the classiest bar in town, but it had been mine for the past fifteen years. I loved being my own boss.

I bought this place to help me find lost souls to save. Demons, vampires and other nasties tend to prey on humans and other creatures in turmoil. The booze was often a magnet for those in need, and I kept a close eye on all my patrons, watching out for someone who needed me. After all, I had to save as many as I had damned in order to get back in to Heaven.

Wow, depressing much?

I studied the riddle on the bracelet. Sometimes Robert's messages were literal, but most of the time, they were exactly what they were intended to be -- confusing. Keying in the entire riddle on my favorite search engine, I began searching the Net. As usual, stupid websites popped up like Porn and Marriage and various book sites with pieces of the phrase woven throughout the story.

Fifty pages later, I gave up and started digging through the stack of newspapers. I combed through every single column from the headlines to the comics. While I did enjoy catching up on my favorite cartoon fat cat, nothing about the riddle jumped out at me. As I didn't have an actual birth date, the horoscopes held little interest for me. Sighing, I pushed away from the desk, glancing at the clock that read eight-thirty. The newspaper was a huge waste of time.

Someone knocked on the door and opened it before I could say come in or stay out. Country music blared from the jukebox located on the wall by the dining tables. I grimaced, grateful my office was soundproof.

A woman wearing a white t-shirt and black pants filled the doorway, holding an empty serving tray in her left hand. Her dark blonde hair was pulled up into a ponytail, and her makeup was laid on a bit heavy – bright red lipstick and too much rouge.

"Hey, Mina," I said.

The waitress placed her right hand on her hip. "Darcy called in sick – again, and I'm supposed to be leaving early, remember?"

Shaking my head, I stood. "One more time, and she is gone. I don't have time to keep filling in for her. I have orders to place, bills to pay and too many patrons to have just one waitress."

I followed the waitress out into the bar, closing the door to my office. To my right were thirteen black round dining tables. Red cloth napkins were set at each place, and a red, glittery poinsettia decorated each table. A middle-aged couple sat at one, and a black-haired young man sat at another. All of the customers in the dining area returned to eat here almost daily.

The area to my immediate left was cleared for traffic to and from the kitchen. A little further down was the bar. One of the regulars, a grey haired man, sat on a stool closest to me, and two people were sitting closer to the entrance.

The bartender, Ben, leaned casually against the counter as he chatted with a blonde barfly who sat closest to where I stood. Her low cut shirt barely held her God-given attributes. I expected one to pop out of her flimsy red dress and poke Ben in the eye. Of course, he was probably hoping that would happen as well.

The music blared from the jukebox, which was located to my right past the tables. Seconds later, the music stopped, and customers' voices blasted the sudden silence. Everyone quickly adjusted his or her pitch to accommodate the lack of noise, and I realized the jukebox had been turned up too loud, and the antique machine needed adjusting. It was a wonder anyone could even understand each other when the music played.

I made a beeline for the bar, intent on asking Ben for help with the jukebox, and entered the bartender's area behind the serving counter. He immediately pushed away from the counter and stood straight.

His chestnut brown hair reached his shoulders, and he tossed his head back to shake the bangs out of his eyes. He had an aristocratic air about him – from the line of his nose to the way he held his shoulders back. His naturally pouting lips curved up into a smile.

"Heya, boss lady."

"Hey. Darcy called in again, so I'm here to lend a hand. Would you please fix the jukebox so it doesn't play so loud?" I asked.

Ben nodded. "Yep. Watch the bar, and I'll take care of it."

Raising my left arm, I showed him the bracelet. "I got a riddle," I whispered. "We need to get the angel patrol together soon."

He patted my hand and smiled. "No worries. We'll help you solve it."

Feeling a tad better, I visited each customer, refilling drinks and making small talk. After gathering a few empty glasses, I looked toward the jukebox to see if Ben was done. He hovered over the machine as if trying to decide what song to pick.

The bells above the front door jangled as a new customer entered. The cross-shaped cat tattoo on my right breast flared with heat, and the cat inside the cross scratched at my skin. Apparently, the new patrons hit Ben's radar as well because his head snapped up, and he looked over his shoulder toward me and the entrance.

Ben raised his right fist, twirling his fingers and bringing forth shadows from behind the jukebox. The darkness swarmed like fog and covered him, obscuring him from sight. Slowly, I faced whatever it was that had my angel-senses on overdrive and had Ben using his vampire powers in front of customers.

Two women and a man stood just inside the entrance. The young man had a buzz haircut, and he wore a button down, striped gray shirt and blue jeans. He kept his gaze on the floor with his thumbs in his front pockets.

The females were twins, and the undeniable scent of vampire poured from them. I wrinkled my nose at the smell of rotting human blood coursing through their veins. It had a touch of copper scent that was quickly fading, and I knew it wouldn't be long before they needed to feed again to keep the old blood from smelling like rotten meat.

Ben refused to drink human blood, but the animal blood he consumed daily still caused a stench. He constantly munched on parsley, but he also brushed his teeth with a mixture of parsley, baking soda and peroxide.

The female vampires haughtily surveyed the place. Both had raven colored hair. One was decked out in Goth clothes complete with black lipstick, eye shadow and nail polish. The other wore a white and charcoal plaid shirt over a tank top and dark jeans.

I was uncertain what the intentions of these newcomers were. It was possible all they wanted was to eat, drink and be merry, but I didn't like the vibes I was getting. So I tensed in preparation for battle.

As nobody else in the bar paid heed to the twins, I assumed that Ben and I were the only ones who knew they were vampires. The rest of the patrons were all normal humans and clueless.

"You can have a seat wherever you like," I said to them as cheerfully as possible.

The Goth one ignored me but glided past the bar toward the dining tables. The man followed dutifully behind her, and the other female brought up the rear. I pretended to wipe down the bar while watching them pick a table and sit. The man briefly glanced at a menu before giving his order to Mina, but the females didn't want anything.

Continuing to take care of the customers at the bar, I knew Ben wouldn't show his fangs until the other vampires left. From the excess of shadows around the jukebox, I knew he hovered in that area.

As I turned to pull a fresh bottle of whiskey from the shelf behind me, the entrance door opened again, and two men entered. They took a seat at the bar right by the door. After I refilled a few drinks, I headed over to the newcomers.

The older man had a salt and pepper beard. Handsome in a rugged sort of way, he wore a black cowboy hat and duster. His companion had his back to me.

I smiled at the older fellow. "What can I get ya'll?"

"Whiskey." The man's gravelly voice sounded weary.

The younger man whirled around on the stool. He had short, spiky blonde hair and a warm smile that included dimples. All he needed was a shave for him to qualify for the boy next door.

Our eyes locked, and his cerulean blue ones pulled me in and held me tight. My breath caught in my throat as my voice disappeared. For a second, time stood still as our souls connected in that infamous instant attraction. The cat inside my tattoo warmed comfortably, and I thought I heard her purring.

He licked his sensuous lips, and a flame of lust shot straight to my nether regions. An image popped in my head of tangled legs and crumpled bed sheets. I placed both hands on the cold green marble counter and did my best to appear unaffected.

"What'll it be?" I asked. I had spent fifteen years as a human, and while I'd had boyfriends on earth and in other realms, the cat tattoo had never reacted like that.

He crossed his arms and tilted his head. "How about a Kiss in the Dark?"

***

CHAPTER 2

The Lusty Crow
Watson, LA
Sunday, December 17th, 9:00 PM
Countdown: 14 Days 18 Hours 59 minutes 59 Seconds

While a kiss from the stranger would satisfy the lust-demon on my shoulder, it would infuriate my parole angel. In no way could I divert from the set of rules I had to follow in order to get back into Heaven. Giving into lustful emotions would not do. Besides, I couldn't let this guy's devastating handsomeness get the upper hand of me.

"How about a Bitch Slap instead?" I tilted my head and smirked. "Or maybe a Vampire's Kiss?"

He leaned forward and placed his arms on the counter, staring intently at my mouth. "On second thought, give me a French Kiss."

The thought of his tongue twirling with mine made my mouth water, and my heart skipped a beat. I pushed away from the counter. "One martini, coming up."

"Don't forget that shot of whiskey," said the man with the salt and pepper beard.

"You got it," I replied.

I turned my back on them and worked on their drinks, but even though I was at the other end of the bar, I could hear the two strangers whispering. I loved having the ability to eavesdrop from a room or two away, especially as the blonde fellow had my lust meter on edge.

"Jack, you better tone it down a notch," warned the older man.

"I know what I'm doing, Dusty."

"Humph. That remains to be seen."

I quickly set Jack's drink in front of him along with another shot of whiskey for his friend. They paid me just as the patron beside them ordered a drink that required fresh lemons. While cutting up a lemon, I tried to ignore the feeling that Jack was watching me, and as I continued to slice with the knife, I chanced a quick glance over my shoulder at him, but he stared above my head at the flat screen TV.

The knife sliced into the finger on my left hand, and biting pain shot through me. I yelped, and blood gushed out of the deep gash. I thought I saw bone. Fortunately, my hand was over the plate, so no blood got on the counter. I grabbed a white towel and wrapped it around my wound.

I looked at the vampires, afraid they might try something with the scent of fresh blood. Fortunately, they were focused on their male meal.

"Are you okay?" Jack asked.

I faced him and pasted a smile on my face. "I'm fine. It was just a nick."

"Are you sure? It looked pretty deep from here. It might need stitches. Let's get you to the emergency room."

"I'll be fine." I grabbed the plate of bloody lemons and dumped them in the garbage can. Setting the plate in the sink, I turned my back to Jack. I dropped the now-red towel into the sink and ran cold water over my finger.

The skin magically closed up, as if some unseen doctor sewed it up with invisible stitches. It still amazed me to watch myself heal, usually instantly. When the cut was gone, I grabbed a band aid from under the counter, stuck it over my finger and began serving customers again.

A heavy set man and a skinny woman entered and took a seat at the bar. The pale woman rested her head on her right hand. Just as I approached to take their order, she spewed her stomach contents all over the bar. I jumped back, thankful none of the vomit had hit me.

"Oh God," she moaned. "I'm so sorry. I told him I didn't feel well enough to go out."

"It's okay." I grabbed a nearby towel and began cleaning up the mess. Fortunately, it was mostly liquid.

The man threw a few dollars on the counter and stuck his business card in one of the fishbowls on the bar. Without a word, he escorted her out. I sanitized the entire area as nearby patrons moved further away.

Once that task was done, I took the man's business card out of the fishbowl. Sometimes I used the cards to find lost souls to save. Mostly I gave away a free lunch, and this couple would be today's lucky winner. I felt sorry for the sick woman.

All the customers appeared to be content and in their cups. I stepped back from the bar and leaned my back against the counter. This position gave me a better view of everything. As casually as possible, I surveyed the entire bar.

The vampires and their male companion began dancing, with him sandwiched between them. Each vampire had her lips pressed against his neck. He faced me, and his closed eyes and contented smile reflected the pleasure their bite gave him.

My anger flared. *How dare they take blood under my roof?*

There were only a handful of customers at the bar, and they were all taken care of at the moment. I tossed the towel in the plastic container under the sink and made my way to the dance floor. I cautiously approached the trio and waited. The man had his back to me, and while the Goth vampire hugged her chest to his, she kept her eyes closed. When none of them acknowledged my presence, I cleared my throat.

The vampiress' eyes opened languidly. The pure black pupils had a thick red border, and red streaks trailed out into the white area. She slid her lips from his neck, pulled her fangs from his skin with a sickening pop and slowly licked the drops of blood off his neck. The holes healed instantly.

"What?" she asked. The three continued to sway to the rhythm of the music playing — *Sitting on the Dock of the Bay.*

"You need to leave." I crossed my arms, forcing down the desire to kick their rancid asses.

"But we're not ready." She pouted.

Her voice rolled over me like liquid chocolate, and I blinked, forgetting why I had approached them. A split second later, my memory returned, and anger replaced confusion. Narrowing my eyes, I shook my head free of the clingy vampire cobweb, and I took a step back.

My first reaction was to make her pay for trying to force her vampire-will on me. However, common sense got the better of me.

I needed to defuse the situation without upsetting the normal customers. Monsters did not exist in their normal world. Tonight wasn't the night to give them an education either.

"I tell you what," I said, spreading my hands in a non-threatening manner. "If you leave willingly, I won't follow you and stake your sorry hearts in the morning."

Goth Girl tossed back her dark hair and rolled her eyes. "Psht, as if you could."

The country vampire stepped away, meticulously dabbing at the corners of her mouth with a napkin. Cameo earrings with a red rose embedded in pewter silver swung from her delicate ears, and a pewter silver chain lay flat against her throat.

"Marishka, let's go."

14

"But, Trina," the Goth one whined.

"I said let's go." The firmness in the country vamp's voice boded obedience. The other vampire pouted, grabbed the man's hand and stomped toward the door.

"I'm sorry for letting blood in your … house." The country vamp held out her left hand. "Thank you for not causing a scene."

I stared at her hand, not wanting to accept it, but I did. She pulled me close, and her warm breath hit my ear. "By the way, *your* blood smells divine."

Okay, *that* crossed the line. I squeezed her hand as hard as I could and felt bones crack. Forcing her down on her knees, I leaned in to her ear this time. The voice in my head warned me to keep her fangs as far away from my neck as I could, which I did as much as possible.

"You really don't want to mess with me. Stay out of my bar and away from me. Or I'll make more than your fingers pop off."

Releasing my grip on her hand, she tumbled back onto her butt. Shock flitted across her face as she quickly she jumped to her feet. The blackness of her pupils swirled red. She lifted her chin and pointed a well-manicured finger at me.

"Watch your back, angel."

Backpedaling her way to the exit, she kept eye contact with me until the door closed between us.

I looked at Jack and Dusty, who had apparently watched the whole thing with intense curiosity. My eyes locked with Jack's. His luscious mouth had turned into a frown, and the intense glare in his eyes wiped away his earlier friendliness.

What the demon wings was his problem?

***

The Lusty Crow
Watson, LA
Sunday, December 17th, 10:00 PM
Countdown: 14 Days 17 Hours 59 minutes 59 Seconds

The bracelet vibrated against my skin. Startled, I stared at the red-glowing words. *Seriously? Had I really let the first clue to the riddle walk right out the door? And why did this stupid bracelet wait until they left before letting me know? Maybe the batteries needed replacing.*

I looked at the bar, and my eyes met Ben's. He was back to his bartending duties after avoiding the twin vampires, which meant I could go after them.

"Be back in a few," I whispered.

Ben nodded, and I went to my office, ignoring the feeling that Jack was watching my every move.

After putting on my black leather riding jacket, I unlocked the bottom desk drawer and pulled out a Walther PPKS .22 handgun. It fit comfortably in my hand, and the stainless steel was overlaid in a special silver coating to keep supernatural beings from picking it up. Of course, they could always use a towel, but I wasn't into overthinking it. In the heat of a fight, I would bet that my opponent wasn't going to be wondering where a cloth was if they tried to take my gun. Tucking it into the holster inside my left boot, I grabbed my helmet and keys and slipped out the back door. My concealed handgun permit was under the seat of my bike along with my driving license.

I hoped I wasn't too late to catch up with the vampires, who were, according to my magical bracelet, a lead in solving the riddle.

My Harley low-rider motorbike was parked right next to the door. I tugged on my helmet and slid onto the seat.

After pushing the kick start, the black-colored bike purred to life.

Quickly checking the half-filled parking lot, I didn't see the twins or their meal. Thus I assumed they had left. I eased the bike to the road and looked left and right. Red tail lights glared from a car that quickly sped away.

I wasn't sure whether it was the vamps or not, but as it was all I had, I turned right onto Highway 16 and zoomed past the only other buildings on this stretch of highway.

The Golden Goose and The Last Resort Bar & Grill were on the same side as my bar. On the other side of the highway was The Lucky Dog Truck Stop, and it had a couple of eighteen wheelers in the parking lot. This part of Watson was pure country, and our little cluster of establishments was the last of the restaurants and gas stations for at least 40 miles going north.

Following the red taillights of my prey, the next three miles were smooth and steady. Only a few vehicles passed, and when the car turned left onto a dirt road, I pulled to the side of the road, cut off my lights and eased up to where the car had turned.

Two metal bars as thick as a barrel were chained together and stopped me from proceeding. Confused, I tried unsuccessfully to see down the dirt road.

How had they gotten through this makeshift gate so fast?

Several old, strong vamps could have levitated the car over the barrier, but I didn't think the twins fit into the category of *old and strong*. Trees lined the dirt rode almost right up to Highway 16, which is why I hadn't seen the makeshift gate until I was right up on it.

A large sign by the highway stated that the property belonged to a local dirt company. Many 'No Trespassing' signs were scattered everywhere. The dirt road led into darkness, but even with my night vision, I couldn't see far. Had someone placed a glamour spell on it to keep nosy people out?

Since I didn't have psychokinesis and the brush on either side was too thick to force my way through, I pushed the kickstand down and eased off the bike. Removing my gloves as I approached the gate, I inhaled the cold night air to help clear my thoughts. The metal chain froze against my flesh as I took it between my palms and snapped it in half. It hit the ground with a loud and lengthy clank, and I clenched my teeth at the noise.

Bright white lights washed over me. To my right, a car had rounded the curve on the Highway and gunned the engine. I covered my eyes with my right hand and squinted. When the top of the car started flashing red and blue, I groaned.

I so don't need the cops butting in right now.

The car pulled over in front of me, and I resisted the desire to bolt. I hoped I didn't get arrested for trespassing. Though technically, I hadn't stepped past the makeshift gate.

The officer opened his door and used it as a shield while he assessed the situation. "Ma'am, is everything all right here?"

I faced him with my hands in clear view. "Yes, sir. I'm just looking for my dog. I thought I saw her run down this road."

"Well, you do realize that's private property? If you go past their gate, it's trespassing, and I'll have to arrest you."

I slowly stepped away from the makeshift gate, hoping he didn't see the broken chain pooled on the ground. "I understand, officer."

Leaving his door open, he walked up to me. "Can I see your license, proof of insurance and registration, please?"

"Yes, sir." I did my best not to sound or act aggravated while retrieving the requested information from a compartment in the bike. I handed the documents to him.

After looking them over, he took my stuff to his vehicle, where I was certain he was checking me out on the FBI's National Crime Information Center data base. That didn't bother me. I had a clean record. However, the pressing matter of solving the riddle did worry me, and the vampires' trail grew colder with each passing minute.

Twenty minutes later, the officer came back and handed me all my paperwork. "Well, Miss, you check out fine. Do you have a picture of your dog? I can take a look for you, but you'll have to go on your way."

"I can text one to you." I put the paperwork back and retrieved my phone. Pulling up a photo of my best friend, I entered the officer's phone number as he dictated it to me. I sent the dog's picture to him so he could pass it around and keep a look out. "Thank you for your help, sir."

"My pleasure, ma'am."

Strapping on my helmet, I straddled the bike and revved up the motor. Easing onto the Highway, I headed back toward the bar. Frustration hummed through me. I had lost my only lead.

Pulling into the empty parking lot of The Lusty Crow, I parked close to the front entrance. Ben had taken charge and closed up the bar for me.

Had time passed that quickly? Was it really 1:30 a.m.?

Turning off the engine, I remained on the bike and stared at the street, wondering how I was going to find those vamps now. I toyed with the bracelet, tracing the words with my right finger.

A black dog half the size of a Shetland pony appeared on the other side of Highway 16. She sat down and proceeded to lick her paw nonchalantly. I shook my head and smiled wryly as I got off the bike and approached the highway. "You were watching the whole time with the cop, weren't you? Would it have killed you to show yourself to get me off the hook back there?"

When I got to the dog's side of the road, I knelt on the shoulder's gravel, removed my biker gloves and rubbed the top of the dog's head. She pulled her head back and away from my hand. My best friend was a weredog, and I knew she wasn't amused. She hated it when I treated her like a real dog.

I didn't hear the screeching of tires until it was too late. The front bumper moved in slow motion against my legs. Bone crunched, and pain exploded through my body. I tried to shove the dog out of the way, but we ended up in a tangled mess. With the huge dog in my arms, I curled around her as we flew back, closing my eyes against the spinning world. My stomach churned with sudden nausea. Landing in the grass, I rolled down into the dry ravine. Stunned, I stayed in a fetal position as pain got the best of me. Kate whimpered and remained unmoving as well.

The car's motor idled. At first, I thought the driver was coming to help us, but then I heard wicked laughter. The cross on the swell of my right breast burned, and the bracelet warmed.

Vampire skanks ... nice job cloaking your approach.

The twin vampires had caught me off guard, which meant they had to be ancient to be able to hide themselves and a 1968 baby blue Ford Mustang.

The pain in my legs faded as the bones mended together. Seconds later, I began crawling up the ravine, mad as hell.

How dare they try to kill me!

Just as I got close enough to see the driver's fang-filled smile, the car's engine revved before squealing away. Dust and debris flew everywhere.

Kate limped up and collapsed beside me. She whined, and when I put my hand on her head, her tail thumped lethargically.

She definitely doesn't feel well if she's letting me treat her like a dog.

I stood, realizing I had lost my left boot. The PPK gun remained tucked in its holster, and I cursed for not having time to pull it out and shoot. Although, the loudness of the shot might have drawn unwanted human attention.

My favorite pair of black jeans hung in tatters from my hip to my calf. Both of my palms had been shredded but were now healed. However, my blood had pooled onto the pavement.

Oh, damn. Let's send out a calling signal for Diabolus' everto canis. Satan's demon dogs were on a mission to hunt down fallen angels, and I really did not need one more thing to worry about. My blood had angelic properties mixed in with the human part, so the dogs would find me.

After finding my lost boot, I picked up Kate, limped across the street, and stepped onto the bar's darkened front porch.

Jack sat on a wooden bench by the entrance. He had his head down as he played with his cell phone.

I froze as my lust meter revved up. *How much had he seen?*

***

Scorned

CHAPTER 3

The Lusty Crow's Front Porch
Watson, LA
Monday, December 18ᵗʰ, 2:00 AM
Countdown: 14 Days 13 Hours 59 minutes 59 Seconds

"Hey." My voice shook despite my attempt to appear casual.

I stood at the top of the porch's stairs, holding Kate's large dog-shaped body. My fingers nervously rubbed the soft fur of her coat, and it seemed to sooth not only her but me as well.

Jack looked up, and the cell phone light splayed across his face. "Hey."

Even though the porch lights were off, there was still light from a few streetlamps. He took in my disheveled state and the dog and jumped to his feet. "Are you okay? What happened?"

"I hit her with my bike," I said.

His boots clunked against the porch as he hurried to where I stood. Taking the dog from me, he laid her out on the porch's floorboards, holding her head in his hand. "Can you make it to the bench while I look her over?"

"Yep," I replied and limped to it. By this time, though, I could have walked normally thanks to my wonderful healing ability. However, since Jack did not know of this power, I needed to keep up the pretense of being somewhat hurt.

"Are you okay?" he asked, leaning over Kate.

"I'm fine." I sank onto the bench.

23

"You don't look fine..." He laughed nervously. "Well, you do look *fine*, but you need to see a doctor. Let me take you to the emergency room."

Shaking my head, I toyed with the edge of my shirt. "Seriously ... I just need a moment to get my nerves settled."

Jack ran his hands over the dog, checking her legs. "She seems to be ok."

Kate lifted her head and licked his face. She struggled to her feet and took off across the porch and into the woods behind the bar.

Smart dog. I wouldn't want to try crossing the street again either.

"Well," he drawled. "Guess she had someplace to be."

Jack walked over to me, knelt, and checked my bones to ensure they weren't broken. He briskly rubbed each of my hands, and the warmth of his touch eased my nervousness. He inspected my palms, but while the dried blood remained, the scrapes had already healed. I tugged my hands out of his, crossed my arms and shivered.

He sat beside me and pulled me against him. "My body heat should warm you up."

"Thank you," I whispered. My teeth stopped chattering. "Where's your car, Mister ..."

I knew his name from eavesdropping at the bar, but he didn't know that. So I waited for him to fill in the blank.

"Jack. You can just call me Jack. No mister." His cinnamon scented breath fanned my ear.

"Nice to meet you, Jack. I'm Angelle."

I held out my hand, and when he took it in his, the warmth went deeper than mere skin. Distracted, I stared at our interlocked hands, admiring how nicely they fit together.

I reluctantly pulled mine from his. Clearly getting hit had affected me more than I thought. Why would Ben let a stranger loiter when he was closing up the bar? "So why are you sitting on the porch after hours? Is my bartender still here?"

Jack shook his head. "No, he left a while ago. We were at the truck stop over there, but I saw him leave." He pointed at the lit up gas station down the road.

An owl hooted in the distance as he shifted. "Well, Dusty and I got into a fight, and he left me across the street. I walked over here, thinking someone might still be inside, but when nobody answered the door … I was trying to call a cab when you walked up."

"I can take you wherever you want, if you don't mind riding on the back of my bike." The comfort of his embrace kept me from moving, and I imagined him leaning in to kiss me. I shook the unbidden thought away.

Tires on pavement hummed in the distance, cutting through the chirping crickets. Seconds later, lights appeared to our left as a vehicle traveled in our direction. It slowed, and the anonymous black hulk became a truck which turned into the parking lot and took a spot next to my bike.

Jack released me from his embrace and stood. "Well, I guess Dusty cooled down."

He took a few steps toward the truck before spinning back to face me. "Are you sure you don't want to go to the ER?"

Grabbing my boots, I stood and shook my head. "I promise you I feel fine. I was going to clean my scrapes here, but I think I'm gonna go home."

Dusty got out of the truck and stepped on the porch. "What's going on? Ma'am, you look like hell."

I raised my hand in a wave. "I'm fine. My injuries look worse than they are."

"Well, at least let me help you to your bike." Jack strode back to me and slipped his arm around my waist.

"No, I can manage," I protested.

I started toward the parking lot, and while Jack had removed his arm, he stayed close. "Are you sure you feel well enough to drive your bike home? I'm sure we can load it in the truck."

Rolling my eyes, I moved past Dusty. "Thanks, but you can't just load a Harley in the back of a pickup truck."

Something stung the back of my neck, and I slapped at the mosquito with my left hand. Instead of a squishy insect, my fingers collided with a dart. I pulled it out, looked briefly at the tiny thing, and slowly turned to face the men.

Dusty pointed a dart gun the size of a deck of cards at me. His lip curled up in a sneer, and he glared at me.

"Dusty," Jack hollered. "No!"

"What have you done to me?" I asked.

Cold ice swept through my veins. My vision swam, and the world tilted dangerously to the left. The boots in my right hand fell as I reached out to stop myself from falling, but all I managed to do was hit my elbow on the bench as I went down.

Dusty knelt over me and held up the dart gun. "Elephant tranquilizer."

I fought to stay conscious.

"Sorry, sweetheart, but I can't allow a vampire to live," he muttered just before I slipped into the dark abyss.

***

Somewhere in the Woods
Watson, LA
Monday, December 18th, 5:00 AM
Countdown: 14 Days 10 Hours 59 minutes 59 Seconds

When I woke, I was in the extra cab of Dusty's truck, which bounced every time the tires hit a pothole. As it happened to be every few seconds, I figured that we were on a dirt road.

Are you freaking kidding me? They're arcane hunters. Good job at spotting fanatics, Angelle. You know those types go off half-cocked and ready to kill anything that isn't human just for that reason alone. Super.

My chest constricted painfully. I couldn't move, couldn't open my eyes, and couldn't even speak. *What the demon-wings had he injected into me?*

My heart raced as fear raised its ugly head. These two intended to kill me, and I had no idea how they planned on doing that. They could've staked me back at the bar, but maybe they didn't want to risk someone seeing. I knew whatever they planned wouldn't work but would hurt like Hell. Being in pain sucked.

Suppose they pierce the vial in your tattoo?

Ice shot through my veins but did little to help my ability to move my body. The acid in my stomach curdled. The cat's poison in the vial would stop my heart instantly and painfully.

The truck suddenly stopped.

"You get her while I get the stuff to tie her down with," Dusty instructed.

The truck shook as he exited. A second later, the extra cab door creaked open, and cold air rushed over me along with Jack's cologne. He gently pulled me out and cradled me in his arms. My head fell back, and my arms hung down. My eyes remained closed despite my attempts to open them. The toes on my right foot wiggled.

Yes! Can't wait to kick your ass, Dusty...

A fresh scent from nearby pine trees cleared my head a little, and as Jack laid me on the ground, leaves crinkled beneath me. A hammer thudded against wood, and not long after, someone wrapped ropes around my wrists and ankles and stretched my limbs out.

"Why can't we just stake her and be done with this?" Jack asked.

"I like to watch them burn." Dusty's voice held entirely too much pleasure at this.

Oh great. A masochist. I cringed at the thought of flames consuming my body, and my heart constricted in fear.

Leaves crunched under their feet, and the sound became distant. My eyes opened a slit. Dusty and Jack stood by the truck, which was about 40 yards to my left. The tree tops whooshed from a sudden gust of wind.

"I can't believe you didn't see her finger heal instantly," Jack whispered. "And when she crawled out of that ditch and walked right up to me ... Proof positive she's a vamp."

You saw that, but you didn't see those twin vampires sucking blood from their victim? Seriously? And the vampires were in the car that hit me.

"Glad yer young eyes are better than mine," Dusty said. He pulled out a cigarette from inside the black duster and lit it up. Smoke swirled above his head. Holding my breath against the fear, I waited for him to come back to me and set me on fire. When he leaned against the truck, I realized he had other plans.

The end of Dusty's cigarette flared red as he took a drag on it. He blew the smoke out of his nose. "I must be getting old. It's getting harder for me to spot the damn creatures."

Jack reached into his pocket and pulled out a pack of gum. As he stuck a piece in his mouth, the scent of cinnamon reached my nose. *Was this a man or a kid?*

"That's why you got me," he said. "I've got yer back."

The dark blue sky began to lighten, and birds started singing their morning song. The warmth of the sun touched my chilled flesh, and I smiled. While I didn't burst into flames, I did get back control of my motor functions. My fingers curled around the ropes that kept me tied to the stakes in the ground.

"Why isn't she bursting into flames?" Jack growled.

"Cuz I'm not a vampire, you dumbass," I said.

I pulled on the ropes, and the hemp bit sharply into my skin. The stakes the ropes were tied to popped out of the ground, and I ripped the rope off my wrists. The ones holding my legs were easier to get free from, and once I did, I threw all of the binding material across the field and over the barren trees.

A vein in my temple beat angrily as my blood pressure skyrocketed. "Time for some payback, boys."

I just wanted to shake some brains into him. Facing them, I saw both had weapons drawn and pointed at me. Having no desire to get shot, I eased toward them. The cold, damp ground seeped through my socks, but I didn't care.

"Where the hell did ya'll get your vampire hunting licenses? The local grocery store?" I snapped.

Dusty pulled the hammer back on the single action revolver. "Take one more step, and you'll see the only license I need is this silver bullet, wolf-bitch."

What the ... so now he thinks I'm a Werewolf? Talk about grasping for straws.

I rushed him because I trusted him about as much as I trusted a demon in a church filled with unrepentant sinners. With my left hand, I grabbed the gun, but it went off just as I twisted it out of Dusty's hand. The bullet slid over the bottom of my forearm and set my skin afire. I bit back a scream and tried to ignore the pain. No doubt, the bullet had been silver, but it didn't affect me as it would a Werewolf. Tossing the revolver to my right hand, I adjusted the gun firmly in my grip.

I moved faster than Dusty and Jack, and they had no time to react. Sweeping my right leg forward, I kicked Dusty's legs out from under him. He hit the ground with a thud and a loud oomph. Placing my socked foot on his back, I kept him from getting up. The humiliation would infuriate him, but I had no choice. I didn't want him attacking me from behind.

Jack took a step toward me, cocking the pistol he held. I pointed the revolver at him, and using my thumb, I pulled back the trigger. "Stop."

He did, resulting in a standoff like the old west.

His jaw clenched. "Not a vamp, not a wolf ... what are you then?"

"What I am is none of your business," I snapped. "How many innocent beings have died because of you two morons? You can't go around just assuming everything must die. You damn arcane hunters need to get a clue, and quit going off halfcocked."

Jack and I made eye contact that resulted in a stare down, and after a few seconds that seemed like eternity, his stance relaxed into a less defensive posture. His blue eyes still eyed me warily, but his lips turned up into a fake smile.

"Well," he drawled. "Maybe we need some educating then."

Did he seriously think I'd fall for that crap? "Save the Southern charm for the tourists."

He took a step back, and his smile faded. "You don't trust me. I don't trust you. Seems we gotta meet somewhere. I'm willing to see what you have to teach me."

His pretty words didn't persuade me to let my guard down. Yet what other choice did I have? I could shoot his foot but risk getting shot too. In order to get them to stop trying to kill me for not being human, they did indeed need some education.

I pressed my foot down just a tad on Dusty's back. "What about you? Are you willing to open your mind to the possibility that other beings aren't all evil?"

Dusty remained quiet. I took his silence as a *no*.

I shrugged. "Your choice. I can't force you. Hey, Jack, do you have any rope left?"

He narrowed his eyes. "For what?"

"Well, for Dusty. I can't let him run lose. A girl's gotta protect herself."

Silence filled the little clearing. Forest sounds surged in my ears. Squirrels barked, and rabbits munched on leaves. Deer miles away stomped through a stream, and a mother coyote growled at her cub.

Certain that neither of them had heard this, I waved my hand at Jack. "Come on. I don't want to be here when that pack of coyotes arrive."

***

CHAPTER 4

Lusty Crow
Watson, LA
Monday, December 18th, 11:30 AM
Countdown: 14 Days 4 Hours 29 minutes 59 Seconds

Turning into the parking lot of the Lusty Crow, Dusty's truck bounced over a few potholes. Ben, Kate and Pete waited on the porch. I had called them on the way with Jack's cell phone, but I couldn't say much more than get your ass to the bar as Dusty and Jack were listening to my every word. I didn't want my friends losing their lives before I could convince the arcane hunters that my friends were playing for the good team. There was no way in Hell I was going to let these two know that they were about to meet more non-humans.

I jumped out of the truck, and gravel dug into my socked feet as I walked across the parking lot. Stepping onto the wooden porch, I shook off the bits of rock clinging to my socks.

Kate tossed her long, raven-black hair over her shoulder and held up my boots. "Lose something?"

"Why'd you leave your bike here?" Ben asked. He stood beside Kate. His eyes held a bit of red, and I prayed he kept his vampire under control. He'd had some Werewolf blood, which enabled him walking in the daylight.

"Thanks." I took the boots and sat on the bench. Removing the wet socks, I donned the footwear. "I didn't

leave it by choice. Those two idiots tried to kill me.
Thankfully, the sun doesn't hurt me. I managed to break
free and *convince* these two to try and open their minds."

Dusty and Jack stood at the bottom of the steps,
looking like they were ready to bolt.

Jack held up his hands. "How many times do I have to
say I'm sorry?"

"A lot," I snapped.

Ben stepped toward them, and I jumped up and
grabbed his arm. He looked down at me. The red in his
eyes deepened, and I shook my head in warning.

"Don't," I whispered. I kept my words below the level
a normal human could hear. To Dusty and Jack, it would
simply appear that Ben and I were having a stare down.

"Hi," Kate said and held out her hand to the two men.
"My name's Kate."

Taking her lead, I made introductions. "Jack, Dusty,
this is Ben and Pete. They help me save lost souls."

After exchanging a doubt-filled glance with Dusty,
Jack held his hand out to Ben, who looked at it as if it
were contaminated. I nudged Ben's elbow, and he shook
hands with a frown.

"Who are they, and why do they need to know about
us?" Ben asked.

I glanced around the vicinity, reluctant to talk more in
the open. Those vampire chicks knew I was onto them,
and the woods across the street could hold any number of
beings sent to spy on me.

"Let's take this inside," I said, heading toward the
door. Ben had already unlocked it and turned on all the
lights. The bar looked different during the day. It felt
cold and empty, and the place smelled like old beer and
stale peanuts.

I took a seat at one of the tables by the office, and
everyone found somewhere to do the same. Jack and
Dusty sat on stools close to the exit. I guess they were

prepared to take flight if necessary. Every one of the angel patrol sat facing them.

"Jack and Dusty are arcane hunters."

A round of groans filled the room, and I held up my hand. "I know. I know, but hear me out. They could have staked me just for being different than other humans, but they didn't. We've reached an agreement, and they're willing to be educated."

"Do they realize *educating* is not a one-time class?" Pete shifted his wrestler sized body around in the chair. He had the face of a Greek god but the intelligence of Einstein.

I met Jack's eyes, and an unexpected flash of heat pooled in my belly.

Really? He tried to kill you, idiot, and you're still lusting after him? Grow up.

"Well, Dusty? Jack?" I asked. "Are ya'll willing to devote a huge chunk of time?"

They looked at each other briefly before focusing on me. Jack cleared his throat. "Tell me what you are first."

Rolling my eyes, I drummed my fingers on the table. To tell or not to tell… "I'm a fallen angel."

"Angelle," Ben growled.

"But I became human to get back into Heaven," I continued.

Jack's jaw dropped, and Dusty quirked his right eyebrow. He leaned forward. "But you're not human."

I held up a finger. "Oh yes I am. My blood is 85% human, and my DNA is the same percent."

Dusty narrowed his eyes, chewing on the inside of his lip. "Humans can die. Apparently, you can't."

His brown eyes never wavered from mine. My lips pursed together, and I sat back in my chair. I wasn't about to tell him that I had an Achilles' heel.

Kate touched the bracelet on my arm. "Another riddle?"

"Riddle?" Jack asked. He slipped off the stool, pushing it close to the bar with his foot. In several strides, he crossed the distance to my table. The chair squealed against the floorboards as he took a seat across from me. "What's that about?"

"Every two months or so, a demon gives me a riddle to solve. If I don't give him the answer in 15 days or less, he takes my soul to Hell." I played with a red napkin on the table.

"Damn, that sucks," he said. He held out his hand. "Can I see?"

Nodding, I turned it so the words faced up. "Ladies in waiting steal gentlemen's port to give to the bride who's forever scorned."

Hesitating, I extended my arm across the table, with my hand palm up. His warm fingers slid under my hand as he leaned closer to see. He traced the numbers as they counted down. "So this reminds you of the deadline."

"Yep," I answered watching over his shoulder as Dusty snorted in disgust.

Sitting on my left, Ben cleared his throat and scooted closer. Pulling my hand out of Jack's grasp, he made a huge pretense of studying the bracelet. He read the riddle out loud. "So any idea what the riddle means?"

"It has something to do with those vampire chicks from last night," I said, pulling my arm free a little more roughly than I had intended. "The bracelet flared red hot heat after I kicked them out of the bar."

"What vampires?" Jack asked.

"The ones you missed while you were drinking at the bar. I mean, seriously. How could you not notice what they were yet mistake me for one?" I rolled my eyes and shook my head.

"We were there when you kicked them out?" Dusty asked.

"Yes," I replied.

Dusty cocked his head to the side. "I don't remember seeing them, and I took note of every single person in the bar."

"But, you both looked directly at me as it happened." My brows drew together. "What were you thinking at the time?"

Jack lifted his shoulders. "I was just wondering when you were going to give me another French Kiss."

"I don't really recall my exact thoughts," Dusty tilted his head as he looked at the floor. "But I did find it strange you stood on the dance floor arguing with yourself."

The twins had cloaked everything they were doing. So that explained how the vampire twins got away with drawing blood in front of humans. Except, they couldn't hide their presence from me or Ben.

"Hang on. I can draw ya'll a picture of them." I went to my office, grabbed a piece of paper and pen, and returned to my seat. Drawing was a hobby of mine, and I quickly sketched out the faces of the vampires. Pushing it in front of Jack, I sat back.

"They're twins. I followed them to the pits but a cop ran me off. I think they're the ones who hit me with their car."

Jack picked up the paper and studied it. He passed it to Dusty and asked, "Isn't this the girl I had to cancel a date with because your ass needed saving?"

***

The Lusty Crow - Angelle's Office
Watson, LA
Monday, December 18ᵗʰ, 12:00 PM
Countdown: 14 Days 3 Hours 59 minutes 59 Seconds

Tossing the sketch of the girl on the desk, Jack sat in the chair and pulled up a website on my laptop. I hovered behind him while the rest of the group lounged around my office. He signed onto FriendlyFace.com, a social networking site.

His picture popped up, and I laughed. Jack was Gothed out with spiked hair, black lips and dark clothes. On his right shoulder was a tattoo of a cross wrapped in thorny roses. I immediately lifted his t-shirt to confirm the tattoo was still there.

"Nice."

He glanced at me, and his baby blue eyes locked with mine. Momentarily captivated, I felt like a rabbit caught in a trap … a really nice trap. The chemistry between us flared. I pushed it down and looked at the laptop screen.

He tried to kill you, girl, my inner voice reminded me.

Um, correction, Inner Self. That was Dusty.

Um, yeah, but Jack didn't lift a finger to stop him …

My inner voice had a way of keeping me straight. I had to admit it helped hold the lust at bay.

Jack scrolled down his list of friends and clicked on a girl. The screen changed to another webpage. Her picture enlarged, and sure enough, it was Marishka. Her black and white page reeked of Goth.

The word 'Trina' filled the screen and dripped red down the page. Beneath the name was a picture of a deathly pale woman dressed in a black Victorian-style dress. Her black hair was draped over one shoulder, leaving the other bare so the two bite marks were visible. The woman looked down, but fangs protruded over her lips.

Oh, how stereotypical. A vamp hiding behind Dracula's shirt tails. Yawn, yawn, save me from the boredom.

When alive, Vlad the Impaler was an evil human perceived as the devil by the people of his time. At the moment, Vlad headed up Satan's torturing department.

My stomach churned at the memory of meeting him, and I pushed the nasty thought away.

"So, Jack, do you think you can try to get her to meet you again?" I asked.

"Let's see," he said and started messaging the vamp.

While Jack worked his mojo on "Trina", I crossed my arms and tried not to stare at the enticing curve of his neck. The sight stirred up thoughts I shouldn't be having if I wanted to get back in Heaven.

I looked at my desk for something to focus on - a glass paperweight with an angel etched inside. A close friend had given it to me as a reminder of my goal - to get back into Heaven, and last time I checked, Lust was not on the list of Holy Virtues.

"Done." Jack sat back, and his hand brushed my jean-clad thigh. "My blind date is tomorrow night."

He rocked comfortably in my chair. I stepped out of reach. While the act might have been accidental, his touch started fires I was determined to extinguish. "Ben, you tail him, and I'll get someone to tend the bar."

The vampire looked up from studying the picture. "Ok."

I placed my hand on Jack's shoulder - big mistake number one. His heat sparked through his shirt, straight up my arm and into my chest. I did my best to ignore it and stopped touching him. "So, do you still have your Goth-clothes?"

He snorted and replied in a low voice, "Only if the people at Glim-Glam Photographers do."

The corners of my mouth lifted, and mirth found a place in my throat. "You went to a makeover photography place? Oh that is awesome."

"Hey, I had no one else to take the picture, and I was sure I'd find some vamps that way." Jack crossed his arms. "Anyway, I can buy some black clothes."

In an effort to ignore my desire, I turned away from him and headed toward the door. "Well, looks like we're going to my fav store."

"Which is?" His voice hovered close behind me. I hadn't heard him leave my chair, which usually squeaked. He was good at maintaining quiet, but wasn't that the way of hunters?

"There's a store in Hammond called Harvey's Angels. They have clothes to help Goth you up. Besides, I need to pick up some things they ordered for me. Be at my house in the morning at nine. I'll text you my address."

Dusty pushed away from the wall where he had been leaning. "I need food and a shower. Let's go, Jack."

I stepped back. Jack's eyes met mine again, and heat flared between us. I looked away awkwardly as he brushed by me.

"Excuse me," he whispered, and I liked the huskiness in his voice.

Rolling my eyes, I took a seat in the chair behind my desk, mentally chiding myself for entertaining having any kind of relationship. *Especially with someone who tried to kill me.*

Everyone left but Ben. He remained seated in the chair in front of the desk, playing with the piece of paper the sketch was on. I waited expectantly.

"What the hell are you doing, Angelle?"

I crossed my arms and looked him in the eye. "What do you mean?"

"Letting these strangers into the angel patrol … I mean, damn. You don't even know them." Ben tossed the paper on the desk angrily.

"True, but you know the old saying … keep your enemies close."

He grunted. "You could have at least consulted us before letting dumb and dumber into the group. I for one don't want to end up with a stake in my chest courtesy of your new fling."

My mouth dropped, and I sat up straighter as anger and embarrassment flared up together. "He is *not* my new fling."

"Right. So I *didn't* see lust in your eyes when you looked at him," he replied flippantly. "You can't get into Heaven with that lust demon you just picked up."

"You're not my parole angel," I snapped. "And last time I checked, *I* was the boss. If you don't like the way I run things, the door's right there."

His chocolate brown eyes swirled red with anger. He jumped up from the chair, knocking it over in his haste and semi-bowed in a curt and completely sarcastic manner. "Yes, ma'am. Next time I'll remember my place."

My shoulders sagged. "Ben, please. I'm not trying to fight with you, but wouldn't it be better to keep those arcane hunters in sight versus letting them run rampant around our city?"

He nodded curtly, refusing to look at me. "You're right. I don't have to like it, but you're right. I gotta go. I just remembered I have something to do before work this evening."

Ben didn't wait for me to respond but stormed out of my office. The door slammed shut behind him.

Great. Now he's mad.

"He'll just have to get over it," I whispered.

My stomach growled, and I headed to my bike, feeling like a cad for not consulting the group before letting in the arcane hunters. I shook my head, reminding myself that I hadn't had a choice. *Besides, you can't please everyone all the time.*

***

CHAPTER 5

Angelle's House
Watson, LA
Tuesday, December 19th, 9:00 AM
Countdown: 13 Days 6 Hours 59 minutes 59 Seconds

Tires crunched over the gravel driveway leading to my house. The vehicle's engine cut off, and the driver's door opened and slammed shut. Standing in the kitchen, I grabbed my purse and smiled in appreciation. It was nice to have someone punctual in the group besides myself.

Peeking through the door's peephole, I ensured there weren't any baddies waiting to jump me. I pulled open the front door. Jack's fist froze in the air. He had been about to knock.

"Too late." I smiled and admired the view.

He looked good enough to scramble up with eggs. Pulling off his sunglasses, he hooked them on the neck of his t-shirt, which showed his muscular biceps quite nicely.

"So, are you ready to go see some motorbikes?" His voice went gruff and sexy, and my insides melted like chocolate chips in a cookie. My gaze lingered on his biceps, and I imagined running my hands over them.

Down, girl. I forced myself to look away, focusing on his black and gray truck in the driveway. I stepped out onto the porch, forcing him to back up. "Let's go then."

Jack followed me to his truck, and we both reached for the door handle at the same time. The heat of his fingers on mine sizzled up my arm, firing up wanton

41

images. Forcing the feeling down, I extricated my hand from underneath his and let him open the door.

As I climbed into the truck, he hurried around to the driver's side. We were soon heading north on Highway 16. I fiddled with the radio and tuned it to a station called The Swamp. They played a good variety of old and new rock, and a Christmas song by the Beach Boy's hummed through the cab.

"Turn right here on Highway 63. We'll take it all the way to Frost," I instructed.

As the truck rolled down the road, I stared at the glove box, wondering what kind of goodies hid inside. Jack reached over and opened it. Packs of gum spilled out onto my lap and the floor. They were all cinnamon flavored.

"I'm a cinnamon freak," Jack admitted.

I raised an eyebrow at him. "Is it gum only or anything cinnamon?"

"Anything … but mostly gum."

An unbidden image of me drizzling liquid cinnamon on his abs played in my head. My throat tightened, and I had trouble swallowing. In an effort to cover it up, I stuffed all but one pack back into the glove box. After handing him a piece, I popped one in my mouth and propped my right foot on the dashboard.

"Hey, I just washed that," Jack fussed.

My foot fell back to the floor. *Can't blame a guy for taking pride ... most guys are fanatics about keeping their trucks spotless. I wonder if he keeps his room this neat. Doubt it.*

"So," I drawled. "Glim-Glam Photography, huh? Not many guys get pictures there by themselves. They're usually dragged there by their girlfriends or wives."

His luscious lips turned down. "Do we have to go over this again?"

I dropped the subject and watched the scenery slide through the passenger window. I let a lot of trees, houses and trailers slip by before speaking again. "So … when'd you get your tattoo?"

Jack hesitated. "Seventeen."

"That's a little young."

He grunted. "So?"

"I thought the law says you have to be eighteen."

He gave me a *'you-know-better'* glance and drawled, "Sure."

I pushed his sleeve up and studied the vines intertwined with the cross. "So who did it?"

"A band of gypsies. They wove a protection spell into it." He glanced at me before returning his attention back to the road.

I tried to figure out where he'd run in to gypsies in Louisiana. The French Quarter in New Orleans was the most obvious place, but it could have been possible that they lived in the swamps.

"I'm joking," He winked at me. "A friend of mine did it at his home. Couldn't do it at his shop ... cuz I was underage. No spell, either."

"It's beautiful. He did a great job. Still, a spell would've been nice." I traced his tattoo, and the heat from his skin seemed to sear through my finger and up my arm. "Why a cross? You don't strike me as an overly religious man."

"Faith was thrust upon me." His words sounded bitter. "I'd rather not talk about it right now."

He turned up the radio, and an invisible shield fell between us. That was my cue to quit poking into his past. I crossed my arms, refusing to get irritated at Mr. Killjoy. *I was just making conversation.*

Chewing on my lip, I snuck a peek at him. The morning sun played over his freshly shaven face, and I became mesmerized. A few seconds later, I forced myself to quit staring at him, even if it was out of the corner of my eye.

What are you doing, Angelle? my inner angel asked.

Apparently, playing with fire.

I let out the breath of air I'd been holding, setting my resolve back in place. *Keep your eye on the goal – Heaven. Not on the distraction.*

I couldn't afford to get sidetracked, even if it was with eye-candy. Jack had dropped into my life, but that didn't mean I had to forego all my goals to play footsies with him. Relationships take time.

Rolling my eyes, I shook my head. *Relationship? Stop thinking in the clouds, and get your mind back in the game, Angelle.*

Toying with the bracelet on my arm, I cleared my throat. "So how long have you and Dusty been hunting together?"

With his left hand resting on the steering wheel, Jack scratched his chin with his right. "Probably about thirteen years now."

"And how does a typical hunt go for ya'll?" I played with the bracelet on my arm.

"What do you mean?"

"Do ya'll have a certain area ya'll hunt, or do you go where the wind blows you?" I asked.

He shrugged. "Depends. Sometimes we get tips or just hear about strange things happening."

"What's the worst …" I hesitated, unsure of what word to call my fellow non-human beings. "Hunt you've ever had?"

Jack tilted his head to the right and made a gulping noise. He paused for a long time, clearly trying to pick from the memories. He turned the radio down. "The first time I went on my own."

I nodded. "Yeah … I'm sure it was terrifying."

"And then some … it was a nest of vampires. Dusty had a family reunion in another state. I stumbled onto them by accident. I had no idea the single vampire I'd been following was headed back to her family of twenty."

My eyes widened, and I whistled. "Twenty vampires? You're lucky you still walk in the sun."

"Very, but I had a good teacher and a few tricks up my sleeves. All but one now lies in a heap of dust." His mouth set in a grim line, and a muscle in his cheek twitched.

I waited for him to continue, but after a few seconds of silence, I suspected there was more to the remaining vampire than he wanted to share. I refrained from pushing him further. Everyone has baggage, and having more of my fair share, I respected his privacy and stopped digging. If I was meant to know the mystery behind the living vampire, then he'd tell me in time.

***

Harvey's Angels
Hammond, LA
Tuesday, December 19th, 10:15 AM
Countdown: 13 Days 5 Hours 44 minutes 59 Seconds

"I refuse to wear leather pants," Jack stated adamantly.

I dropped the pair of black leather pants over my arm. "Excuse me, princess, but they're for me ... not you. There's a rack of jeans for guys over there. You *can* shop for yourself, right? Or does dear old mom still pick out your clothes?"

His face darkened, and he abruptly moved away without a word. *Oops. Stepped on toes there. Note to self – don't pick on him about his mom.*

Standing at a rack, I pushed clothes around, pretending to be engrossed. I watched Jack as he dug through the men's selection. If what he picked didn't measure up to my standard of Goth, then I would step in. When he at last came back, I had already agreed with the choices he had made – a long-sleeved black shirt with matching denim boot cut jeans and jacket.

"I don't suppose we have an expense account," Jack said.

I rolled my eyes up to look at his face. "I didn't know you were such a comedian."

"That's what I thought. Don't we have a SuperMart in Baton Rouge? Wouldn't it have been cheaper to go there?"

"We do, but those general stores don't have quality clothes. You need to make an impression on this *Trina*. We need to give you a complete makeover in case she remembers you from the other night. It's possible she saw you sitting at the bar."

I turned to go to the counter and almost knocked over the sales girl. "Jeneen. I am so sorry."

The brown haired woman was two inches shorter than myself and thin as a post. She wore clear latex gloves because she was allergic to practically everything. I shopped here a lot and had become friends with her a long time ago.

"Hey, Angelle," Jeneen said. "I'm okay. How've you been? Haven't seen you in forever."

"I've been better." I double checked the store to make sure it was still empty. "Hey, I think my special order is in."

"Let me go check for you," Jeneen said and headed toward the Customer Service desk.

"Thanks."

Jack followed me to the bike area. "Your bar must make a killing."

"I'm not complaining."

There was no way in Hell I was going to tell Jack about The Human Society I belonged to, nor of its president, Chadwick. Members devoted their lives and souls to the protecting of innocents and also received great benefits, such as six figure salaries and month long, paid vacations. Not that I ever took the vacation. My time was better spent running the bar that attracted lost souls to save, and since I didn't take expensive vacations and saved most of my money, I liked to indulge in clothes.

I handed him the shirts and jeans I intended to purchase and straddled a beautiful bike. Leaning forward, I imagined the wind in my hair. "So what do you do for a living, Jack?"

Jack ran his hand along the chrome handlebars. "I'm in the *of all trades* portion of my illustrious non-career, but fortunately, I'm good at saving for those rainy days. Seems like there's more of them every time I turn around."

Letting go of the handle bars, I leaned back and looked up at him. "I need some help at the bar. Think you'd be interested?"

He tilted his head. "Maybe."

Swinging myself off the orange colored low rider, I crossed my arms. "It pays minimum wage, but it's something to do while you and Dusty get educated. Not to mention it'd be good cover against any baddies that may be lurking around."

"That's a good idea, and I can always use money," Jack said. "What would I be doing?"

"This, that and *of all trades*," I smiled. "It's a bar. I'll let you fill in the blanks."

Jeneen waved at me from the back corner of the store. I glanced at Jack. "I'll be right back, ok?"

"Sure. I'll just look around some more," he said, already moving toward a black motorbike.

I followed Jeneen through a door and down a well-lit hallway. Stopping in front of a wall covered in daisies, she inserted a key into the center of the biggest flower. She pushed the hidden door open, and we went into a 12 by 12 room.

Jeneen walked around the counter to a set of metal shelving. Along the walls on either side of me were weapons – crossbows, bow and arrows, rifles and more. My Walther PPK was safely in my boot where it belonged.

Obviously, the store catered to more than the human customers. The owner wasn't picky about who they were, either. All that was required was passing a background check to ensure the purchaser is not a felon.

I had often considered trying to find his list of clients because I had a sneaking suspicion a few of them were on The Human Society's Most Wanted list. However, the owner, Harvey, helped me out on a regular basis. So I let that sleeping demon lay, so to speak.

I stepped up to the counter as Jeneen began laying out boxes of bullets. They all fit my PPK, but only one box was meant for humans. The rest of the bullets were magically enhanced to take out various nasties. The silver ones were, of course, for werewolves, and the ones for vampires were blessed with holy water. For fairies gone rogue, there was a box of iron bullets. Most of the boxes were bullets dipped in crystal – for demons, as they gave me the most problems. These worked well with demon dogs too.

"Does this look like what you ordered?" Jeneen asked.

I ran my hands over the boxes, strangely comforted by them. "Yep. Ring it up please."

After the business was taken care of, Jeneen handed me the bag of bullets and pointed at the bracelet. "Another riddle? Anything I can help with?"

"Do you know a scorned bride? Or any ladies in waiting?" I took the bag from her and stepped back from the counter.

Jeneen thought for a few seconds, staring out in space. She looked back at me and shook her head. "Nope."

"Oh well, never hurts to ask."

Escorting me out of the room, Jeneen locked the door behind us. "If you need a witch's help, let me know. I pack a mighty mean punch-spell."

I nodded. "Sure thing."

"I'll keep my ears open, though, and I'll let you know if I hear anything," Jeneen said as her heels clicked on the wood floor.

Stepping out of the hallway and into the front area of the store, I caught Jack's eye and pointed to the register. He met us there and laid our clothes on the counter for Jeneen to ring up.

While waiting, I looked at my boot and saw something partially hidden under the bottom edge of the counter. I knelt down and picked up the object. It was a Cameo pendant with a rose embedded in the pewter silver. *The country vampire from the bar was wearing matching earrings.*

Standing, I turned over the pendant. Inscribed on the back was I3413. The bracelet glowed faintly but only for a few seconds. Obviously, I was on to something.

I held the cameo up so Jeneen could see it. "Any idea who this belongs to?"

Taking it from me, she turned it over and over in her latex gloved hands. "A dark haired vampire came in here the other night needing some parts for her bike. It might have belonged to her."

"Really?" I responded. My hopes lifted. "Do you have her address?"

Jeneen shook her head, making her long brown bangs shake. "Nope. If you want, I can remove the gloves and see if I get any vibes from the pendant."

I nodded. "If you don't mind."

She pulled off the glove covering her left hand and dropped the pendant in her palm. Closing her eyes, she appeared to meditate, but I knew that touching objects sometimes gave her visions.

Jack nudged me and whispered, "What is she doing?"

I took a few steps back, pulling him with me. I didn't want to break her concentration. "She has certain … abilities that let her see through the eyes of an object's owner."

He appeared impressed. "She's clairvoyant."

I was uncertain as to how he felt about witches, so I decided to go with his assumption. "Something like that."

Jeneen cleared her throat, and we moved back to the counter. "All I could see was an old, large house."

Handing me back the Cameo, she replaced her gloves and finished bagging up the clothes we had purchased. I tucked the pendant in my pocket.

"Did I mention that the parts she came in for had to be ordered?" Jeneen asked casually.

My ears perked up. "Really? But she didn't leave an address."

"Paid cash."

"What about a cell phone?" Jack asked.

Jeneen shook her head and handed the bag to him. "Said she didn't have one."

"Drat," I said.

"But the parts are in, and she said she'd be here tomorrow evening to pick them up."

Sweet! She'd get more than just parts when she did. She'd get a stake in her chest if I had anything to say about it.

***

CHAPTER 6

Angelle's House
Watson, LA
Tuesday, December 19th, 1:00 PM
Countdown: 13 Days 2 Hours 59 minutes 59 Seconds

Holding a beer in one hand and a glass of sweet
Moscato wine in the other, I used my hip to push open
the screen door leading to the covered back porch. Even
though the sun rode high, the temperature was at a chilly
sixty-eight degrees. Having lived in Hell, I thrived in hot
weather. It's one of the reasons I had chosen to live in
Louisiana. So, consequently, anything below seventy
degrees had me running for a blanket.

I sat next to Jack and huddled around the chiminea.
"Thanks for getting the fire started."

He twisted the top off the long neck bottle and took a
deep swig. "You're welcome," he drawled.

I snuck a peek at him as he stared into the fire. He had
a five-o'clock shadow that added a sexy roughness to his
youthful features.

"So, Jack."

He turned to me, and the sunlight played over his
face. When our eyes met, warm desire flooded over me. I
pushed away the unwanted feeling and looked back into
the fire. It was safer then contemplating my attraction to
him.

"What?" he asked.

"Ben's going to be at the place you're taking your
date … just in case you need backup."

Something stabbed my heart at the thought of him on an actual date with someone else. I looked at his lips, wondering how it would feel to kiss them, and my body warmed down to my toes. Aggravated with my stupid thoughts, I looked the other way.

He tried to kill you.

"Good. We should be at The Last Resort Bar & Grill around 8," he said.

"It shouldn't take me long to get you all Goth'd up. We don't have to get you ready until about 6:30. You can hang around here til then, unless you have some business elsewhere."

He shook his head. "Nothing planned."

"I hope you can get her back here without any problems. Kate and Pete will be here. The minute she steps on my porch, it's all over for her."

Jack cleared his throat and shifted in his chair so that he faced me. "Listen, I'm sorry I tried to kill you."

Shrugging, I picked lint off my sweater. "No biggie. Happens all the time."

I took a sip of wine, and the liquid slid down my throat. "Are you hungry? I can whip us up a mean frozen pizza. Well, it's not actually mean. It's really kinda nice."

His deep laugh sent warm pulses vibrating through me. "Maybe in a little while. I'm enjoying this."

I smiled and couldn't resist another peek at him. He caught me this time, and our eyes locked. Something danced between us, catching us in its magical web. I had trouble remembering why I was resisting the attraction.

Does attempted murder ring a bell? My inner voice asked. *And how about getting back into Heaven?*

When he leaned closer, warning bells dinged in my head. I jumped up and moved to the porch railing, hoping he wasn't trying to kiss me. *I mean, seriously, dude. A simple apology does not mean free access to my lips.*

"Have you been on many blind dates?" I asked.

"Haven't really dated much since --" He paused and cleared his throat. "Well, since I became a hunter." He took a swig of beer. "How about you? Date much?"

I shrugged. "Not really. Too busy dusting baddies and taking care of the bar."

An owl hooted, and the fire in the chiminea popped. Smoke curled out of the top and drifted lazily toward the stars. Truth was, I had only dated a few human men since landing in this realm. Too many bad memories from when I'd been with Nate.

"My top priority has been to catch the vampires that killed my parents," Jack said.

My eyes grew wide as I instantly recalled the comment I had made earlier about his mother dressing him. Crap. "Oh, Jack. I'm sorry."

"It was a long time ago."

He leaned forward and stuck the poker in the fire. The logs hissed, and the flames leaped like dancers with their feet tied to the ground. "Not yet. It's actually them, not him – one female and two males."

"How'd it happen? Or is that a taboo question?"

He finished his beer and set it on the table. "Well, I walked in on the whole bloody massacre. I was seventeen and back from a date. The porch light was out. Knew something was wrong, but I ignored it. When I stepped into the house …"

Pain edged onto his face. I didn't want him to feel obligated to showcasing his memories. "You don't have to go on."

"No, I'm fine. I haven't told anyone this except to Dusty, who taught me how to hunt." Jack leaned forward with his elbows on his knees and stared intently into the fire.

"My mom lay on the couch with her hand reaching out to me, and one of the vampires knelt by her ... sucking on her neck. The female sat on my father's lap, licking his blood off her lips. She'd drained him. Next thing I knew, my gut burned, and when I looked down, my stomach had been ripped open and blood gushed out of me. I looked to my right at a male vampire licking his fingers before I passed out. When I woke, Dusty had stitched me up. He'd dusted the one feeding off me and scared away the other two."

I swiped at a tear and fought to remain composed. He had been just a kid. Words escaped me, and the silence stretched awkwardly around us. When he didn't speak, I glanced at him to ensure he was okay, and I could tell from his gaze that he was lost in some disturbing memories.

A few seconds later, he cleared his throat. "Do you want to see the scar?"

I nodded. He pulled his shirt up, and I knelt beside him to get a better view. The tips of my fingers traced the three jagged scars zigzagging from above his belly button to inside his jeans. Another mistake. My hand burned hotter than the fire, and I snatched it away. Desire made me want to finish following the trail that led to something far more interesting than vampires.

As if scorched, I jumped to my feet, finally finding something to say. "Pizza time."

He followed me into the kitchen and helped me fix the pizzas. We made idle chit-chat about what his duties might be at the bar, and before long, we were back on the porch with the food.

After the hunger beasts were satisfied, Jack sat back in his chair with a satisfied grunt. "So what do you do for fun?"

I shrugged. "Watch TV or movies. If I'm not riding my Harley, I like to go horseback riding on the weekends. A friend of mine in Springfield has about a dozen horses. His wife died a few years ago, and I helped him teach his little girl to ride.

"Can angels have kids?"

The question came out of nowhere and threw me for a loop. I didn't want to tell him about my past yet, but he had given me something from his.

"Angels cannot have kids, but fallen angels can. I have a son from my ex, but I never hear from that kid. He's all grown up and on his evil own now."

Jack's eyes widened as he looked me over from head to toe. He whistled. "You are definitely one hot looking mom."

"Thank you, but before you entertain lascivious thoughts about me, you should know that when I was in Hell, I was over the lust demons, and in order to get back in to Heaven, I can't have premarital sex."

He tilted his head. "Lust demons?"

"Yeah, they're the ones who get people in trouble, especially married people and sex addicts." I touched his hand, and the physical connection between us flared. The pupils in his eyes were dilated, which meant he felt the attraction too. "So, do you still want to think dirty about me knowing I tangled with demons?"

"Maybe." His voice was serious and dead sexy.

My insides turned to liquid. Wiping my mouth, I stood, gathering up the used paper plates and napkins. I turned to go inside, but Jack grabbed me by the waist and pulled me onto his lap. His eyes searched mine.

"What are you afraid of, Angelle?"

Going back to Hell. My mouth dried up instantly, and I couldn't speak.

"Is it this?" He kissed the tip of my nose.

"Or this?" His lips scalded my cheek. I couldn't make a sound, much less gather up the will to move off his lap.

"Or could it be ..."

He made mistake number three for me. He planted a soul stealing kiss on me, and I lost track of all sense of time and reason.

When he released my mouth from his sweet prison, he didn't go far, but held his arms tightly around me. His nose almost touched mine, and his breath feathered against my lips.

"You know I'm stronger than you, and I can easily overpower you," I whispered.

"Yeah, but you haven't." His tongue darted lightly over my mouth.

"But I could."

"You won't." Jack smiled with self-assurance.

Something in his pocket started vibrating, and I quirked my left eyebrow. "Do you do that for all the girls?"

He snickered and released me from his grasp. I scooted off his lap and very far away from him.

"We're not through with this conversation." He pulled his cell phone out of his pocket. Giving him some privacy, I took the trash into the kitchen. His conversation didn't last long, and he trapped me against the counter. "Are you going to answer my question?"

"Which question?"

He pushed my hair away from my neck and kissed my skin. "What are you afraid of?"

In truth, I was scared of a lot of things. I opted for a simple answer. "I haven't been in a serious relationship with anyone for a very long time."

As in thirty years ... as in with Satan.

Understanding lit his face. He looked me over appreciatively. "How have you managed ... especially with that body?"

I smiled, flattered. "Pure determination."

Jack pressed his body against mine, adding number four to my list of mistakes. "I would love to stay and try to persuade you, but Dusty needs help with something. While I appreciate your offer to help transform me into a Goth God, I'm going to have to manage on my own."

Relief and disappointment warred within me as I walked him to the front door and watched him leave. He had tried to kill me, but that excuse couldn't fly anymore, especially since he had apologized. So now, the only thing that stood between me and Heaven (besides the number of souls I had to save) was this lust between Jack and myself. I wasn't so sure I was strong enough to resist it, and that scared the Hell out of me.

***

Angelle's House
Watson, LA
Tuesday, December 19th, 4:00 PM
Countdown: 12 Days 23 Hours 59 minutes 59 Seconds

I doused the dimly lit fire with a few cups of water. I didn't like to take any chances. Fire demons were mischievous, annoying little creatures. They tended to escape Hell often and render terror on unsuspecting humans. I had no intention of becoming one of their victims.

Wings fluttered in my ears. My human eyes saw nothing, but my sixth sense kicked in. I couldn't see the angel as the glory of such a being would permanently blind a mere human. So I waited, wishing I could see the pearlesque wings I used to have.

My heart wept at the sadness of Heaven lost. What a silly angel I had been, but I'd been blinded by love. The most perfect day on earth is but a drop of rain in the ocean when compared to Heaven's worst day. My fallen brothers and sisters had been too spoiled to realize what they … what *we* had as residents of Heaven.

"Hello, Angelle."

"Hey, Cal. How have you been?"

"Could be better if a certain angel would keep her wits about her instead of mooning over some human."

I crossed my arms, pushing down the shame rising inside. "Would you please show yourself so I can quit talking to air?"

The silhouette of a man appeared in a chair to my right. The porch light bathed his golden-hair. His face remained hidden in shadow, but I knew its handsome contours well. I wasn't surprised that my Celestial parole angel, Lecahel, showed up after all the lustful thoughts I'd been having about Jack.

"So, Cal," I started. "I'm not an angel anymore, and I haven't done anything but kiss Jack."

"I know, Angelle. I've come to remind you of the follies of lust."

"Uh, hello? I used to oversee the lust demons. I think I know a thing or two about it."

Cal crossed his arms. "Love, however, is an angel of a different color."

He was right about that. Love didn't have the usual white wings but a lovely shade of pink. Of course, he wasn't being literal.

"I'm not looking to fall in love and get married. My heart belongs to me, Cal. Always has, always will." I crossed my arms in defiance. "Not even Nate had the keys to it. I was young and naïve, and he was my first lesson on lust. Too bad I realized it way too late."

Cal nodded. "Okay. Long as we're clear on the subject."

My patience slipped. "We've been clear since day one, Cal."

"Okay, Angelle. I had to check." His calmness reminded me of still water. "Sometimes one can get lost in the moment and think they are in love when they are actually in lust."

Tired, I wanted nothing more than to climb into a hot tub. I wasn't in the mood for a lecture. "I know I'm in lust, Cal, and I'm being careful. I really am. No wedding, no bedding. I have absolutely no intention of falling in love."

"I'm only a thought away if you need some support."

I yawned. "Is this going to take much longer? Should I get us some food and drink?"

"This is serious, Angelle." Cal's voice boomed like a bolt of thunder. I felt like a child being yelled at by her father. "You're on the right path. Don't let lust de-rail you."

Chagrined, I immediately regretted the cavalier attitude I exuded. I sat in a chair and ran my hands through my bangs. "I'm sorry. You're right. Jack is trouble."

"He's not trouble … unless you let him become trouble. All I'm saying is love doesn't grow in the microwave. It has to cook … slowly … over a low heat."

My head snapped up. "Like I said, I have no intention--"

"No one ever intends to fall in love, Angelle. It just happens."

I stared at him in exasperation. "Are you trying to tell me something here, Cal? Am I going to fall in love with Jack?"

He shrugged. "Only time will tell."

"I don't want that, Cal. No more lust … no more *falling in love*. This girl has had enough of men and their domineering ways."

The old feelings of being in a prison made of love surfaced. Or I should say, made of lust. Satan had done a number on me, and while I hadn't seen him in over thirty years, I was still his victim. I never wanted to feel powerless like that again.

My voice edged with steel. "Don't worry, Cal. You opened my eyes, and lust will not happen in this body. Whatever it takes, I'm going to make sure of that. No more alone time with Mr. Get-Me-Hot-And-Bothered."

Cal stood. "Good. That's all I wanted to hear. Now, if you'll excuse me, I have to take care of a Sangre demon. It seems he has been trying to mate with some humans in order to breed."

Crossing my arms, I wanted to pout, but the desire to help won out. "Be careful. Sangre demons are high up on the hierarchy. They're powerful, and few in ranks."

"Thank you. I will take heed." He vanished with the following words ringing in my ears. "Next time, I'll give you notice I'm coming. I want a piece of your devil's cake. You turned out to be one helluva cook."

"Thanks so much for the visit, Cal. Really appreciate the eye opening conversation."

As soon as Cal left, my cell phone rang. Time literally stopped when Cal visited, but I rushed to answer it.

"I just got through visiting the gravel pits and thought you'd like a re-cap," Ben said. "I didn't find any vampires, but I did find tire tracks leading right into the Amite River. I took a little swim, but there was no sign of a vehicle at the bottom."

Cell phone to my ear, I double checked that all doors were locked before heading to the bathroom. "Good job, Ben. Thank you."

"You're welcome. I'll see you later tonight."

"Yep. Later."

Hanging up the phone, I prepared my bath. When the bubbles reached the edge, I slipped into the tub and rested my head. My eyes closed, and I let my mind drift.

Unbidden, an image of a naked Jack popped into my head. My eyes flew open, and I groaned. It was definitely lust. I was determined not to fall in love. Besides, I had only known him for a little more than day.

Love at first sight.

"Not quite," I said out loud.

I recalled my first meeting with Jack. Sparks had definitely ignited, but I couldn't call it love. Definitely only a case of physical attraction.

61

So why did Cal hint at the possibility of me being in love with Jack?

Because Cal is off his wings.

Jack hadn't done a single thing to earn my love. In fact, he'd tried to fry me in the sun. That should've earned him my undying distrust, if not hate. Strangely, it didn't.

Besides, Angelle, when have you ever known love wait to be earned? Love has a mind of its own.

I sighed and felt a small tremor of fear knock at the edge of my armor. Satan had twisted my love and turned it against me. When I escaped from Hell, I'd been an emotional train wreck. Cal had found me and helped me through that time. I couldn't go through that again. I wouldn't.

But Jack is not Satan. He's human, and on the good side of the fight.

Abruptly, I sat up, pulled the plug and got out of the tub. Drying off, I looked at my reflection in the mirror.

"Enough, girl. The angel patrol will be here shortly. We do have a riddle to solve, and that comes first … or there won't be any of me in this realm to do any falling in love with anyone."

***

Scorned

CHAPTER 7

Angelle's House
Watson, LA
Tuesday, December 19ᵗʰ, 9:00 PM
Countdown: 12 Days 18 Hours 59 minutes 59 Seconds

Kate and Pete stood at the kitchen table with me as we laid out the weapons we planned on using to catch the vampress. We had a pair of silver handcuffs, a few crosses, some garlic and holy water-filled balloons with crosses on them. I loaded the special vampire bullets into my Walther PPK and set it on the table.

"I see Vivian has her own arsenal of weapons," Kate said, nodding toward the tiny birdhouse hanging in a corner of the kitchen.

A kitchen angel lived in my house. I couldn't see her unless I ate a primrose cookie, which caused all sorts of crazy reactions, so I avoided doing so. Vivian and I communicated in odd ways but mostly with notes on the fridge's dry erase board.

"Oh, yeah," I said. "She can hold her own. That's for certain."

Lights flooded the dining room window as a truck pulled haphazardly into the driveway. Just as quickly the lights blinked out, and the loud engine shut off. A door slammed, and footsteps pounded on the porch.

"Demon-wings," I muttered, setting a pack of bullets on the table.

"Is that Jack?" Kate asked.

She carefully set a filled water balloon in an empty egg carton. The holy-water-blessed balloons fit perfectly in the hand, and unsuspecting vampires often had their skin singed with the holy water before getting staked-to-dust.

"I sure hope not. We're not in position," I growled and started toward the front door just as the doorbell rang. I flung open the door.

Jack stood impatiently before me in his black jeans and shirt. His spiked hair had been sprayed black, and he had a spiked collar around his neck with a matching band around his right wrist. My body parts melted at the sight of him, and if I could see the lust demon doing this to me, I would've vanquished the little booger right then and there. As it was, I was caught in the spell it had woven.

Nervously, Jack looked over his shoulder before brushing by me. On his way past, he grabbed my hand and pulled me in with him. He shut and locked the door.

"Are you being chased?" I hoped for a little fight action. I'd take anything to distract me from the heat in his gaze that made me want to forget the goal. "And are they vampires?"

Following him into the kitchen, he stopped abruptly, and I bumped into his back. I stepped back and rubbed my nose. He swung around. "If I'm being chased, it wouldn't be vampires tonight ... more like the cops."

"For what?"

"For having a date with a minor." Jack's face scrunched up, causing his eyes to squint. "For buying said minor a beer ... for kissing said minor in public."

Each time he said *minor*, he pounded his right fist into his left palm for emphasis.

My jaw dropped. "What the hell ..."

Jack's eyes darkened. "My date turned out to be a human - not a vampire like we all thought." He stepped back with clenched fists, and he forced out his words. "A very young, very mature looking human hacker who looked just like our vampire."

Leaning against the door frame, I forced back a smile. "How old?"

"Seventeen. She told me while we were dancing, and then she kissed me. I pushed her back the minute her lips touched mine." He yanked open the fridge door and pulled out a beer.

"Yeah. Hot young girl kissing old coot. I'm sure you weren't busting down the door to get away." I grabbed the bottle out of his hand, put it back and handed him bottled water instead. He didn't need to be drinking and driving.

"Since when is thirty old?" Taking a swig of the water, he began pacing.

"As compared to seventeen?" I raised my left eyebrow. "So tell me. How'd you escape from the teeny-bopper?"

Jack moved to the table and idly picked through the weapons. I could tell he really wasn't looking at the strange array of supernatural-stopping mechanisms. Clearly his frazzled mind was elsewhere.

"I went to the bathroom," he said. "And when I came back, I told the girl I had to leave on an emergency. I escorted her to her car …"

Picking up a water balloon, he tossed it back and forth in his hands. He cleared his throat. "Her mother was asleep behind the wheel."

My laugh busted through my lips before I could stop it. The scene in my head was too funny. "Did you give her a good night kiss?"

Jack rolled his eyes at me. "Wow, you're a comedian."

The doorbell rang, and I continued chuckling as I went to answer it. Looking through the peephole, I saw Ben and opened the door for him. He grinned from ear to ear. "Where's he at?"

He didn't wait for a response but headed to the kitchen. I followed, trying not to laugh out loud.

"Hey, man." Ben's voice was full of held-back laughter. "Are you through babysitting?"

"Shut up," Jack growled.

"Man, you should've seen the look on your face when she told you she was seventeen."

Jack glared at Ben. "How'd you hear that? You were on the other side of the room."

In an effort to help keep Ben's vampire-state a secret, I jumped into the verbal sparring. "Guess instead of backup, I should've sent you with a chaperone."

Ben laughed. "And maybe some bubblegum. Say, man, does she still watch the Disney channel? On your next date, you can take her to Penguin Pete's Pizza Palooza."

Jack grabbed Ben by his t-shirt and threw him against the counter. Jack twisted the vampire's nice button-up shirt. "I have an idea, Mr. Mouth. How would you like to taste my knuckles?"

Surprised that Ben allowed the arcane hunter to get the upper hand, I stepped between Jack and Ben. The hunter's baby blues weren't so baby anymore. They had turned darker, but I wasn't afraid. It's kind of hard to be afraid when you're ten times stronger.

"Stop it, boys," I said and pushed Jack back a step so Ben could move away.

Jack didn't like it one bit, and the air changed from frivolous to menacing. His male pride sprang to the surface, and he wrenched free of my grasp, stalking off into the living room.

"So what do we do now?" Kate asked as she packed up her weapons.

Reaching into my back pocket, I pulled out the rose pendant and showed it to them. "Found this at Harvey's Angels. It matches the earrings one of the vampires wore. Jeneen said the vamp ordered some bike parts that she's picking up tomorrow evening."

Kate took the pendant from me and looked it over. She even sniffed it, and red lines swirled in her green eyes. Her smile seemed more sinister than happy. She tossed the pendant to Pete, and whispered, "I've got her scent now."

He smelled the jewelry as well, and his hazel Werewolf eyes also had red swirls in them. "Want us to track her?'

Jack wasn't in the room, but I knew he heard everything that was said. I made a mental note to talk to Ben, Pete and Kate at a later time about working harder to keep their supernatural state of being quiet. My plan was for Jack and Dusty to get to know them on a personal level before revealing Pete, Kate and Ben's true identities.

"Y'all want to go to the motorcycle shop to wait for her?" I asked and began putting the weapons in the chest in the corner of the kitchen.

"No," Jack said as he appeared in the doorway.

He had taken off the Goth accessories, but he still looked sexy as all get out with his spiked hair and tight fitting clothes. I hoped he would wear them again.

He tossed the water balloon at me, and I caught it, glad it hadn't busted all over me and the table of weapons. I placed it in the egg carton.

"No?" I asked. "Why can't they go?"

"They can go as backup." Jack sighed. "But I'll play the guinea pig."

***

Harvey's Angels
Hammond, LA
Wednesday, December 20th, 7:00 p.m.

Countdown: 11 Days 20 Hours 59 Minutes 59 Seconds

Sitting on the edge of the backseat in Pete's pickup truck, I watched the store's entrance. He and Kate were in there, keeping an eye on Jack. I couldn't go in because the vampires would recognize me. Not that I cared because I intended on dusting their asses the first chance I got. I simply couldn't allow a fight to happen in front of normal humans.

I fidgeted, aching for something to do. Surveillance was not my forte. Adjusting my baseball cap, I draped my arms over the front seat and ran my fingers back and forth over the rough fabric.

Most of the light poles in the parking lot were busted. The remaining handful only gave off a low glow. There were several vehicles around me, but Pete had parked so I could get a good view of the inside of the store, which was lit up like a small city. I could see the people shopping, but they couldn't see me.

My cell phone vibrated, and I pulled it out of my pocket. Kate had sent a text. *Jack's made contact.*

I responded with *Good. Don't let him out of your sight. He's only human.*

Placing the cell phone on the seat, I resumed my vigil of the store. Jack and the vampires walked past the front door and over to the motorbikes. He sat on one while the two vampires hovered on either side of him. Marishka rubbed her hand up and down his bicep while the country vamp pointed at the bike's dashboard and pressed her breasts against his other arm.

I narrowed my eyes, wanting to storm inside and yank both of them away from him. Rolling my eyes, I shook my head. The emotion was absurd. I knew they would be all over him. *So why are you reacting this way? Get over it.*

The trio moved slowly around the store, obviously chit-chatting. I thought about tuning in on their conversation but decided against it. The vamps might be able to sense that someone was using supernatural powers.

Kate and Pete coordinated their movements so that they were always on the opposite side of the store from Jack and his new vampire friends. Pete inspected everything while Kate played the bored girlfriend. Her cell phone never left her hand, and every so often she would text me things the vamps and Jack were saying.

They just told him it's their birthday, and they want to be a cake for him. Gag.

I typed, *Ok, TMI, thanks. Let me know if they say anything riddle-related.*

Kate sent back a smiley face with a tongue sticking out of it. I rolled my eyes, laughing at how cell phones can make people act like kids.

When Jack and the vamps approached the check-out counter, Pete and Kate pushed through the entrance doors and quickly got in the truck. Pulling the bill of the baseball cap down over my forehead, I sat back, trying to meld into the shadows of the truck. "Don't start the engine up. I don't want the lights of the dashboard illuminating anything in here."

Kate remained face forward. "Good idea."

The vamps left the shop, and Jack exited too and stepped up to my motorbike. Against my better judgment, I had agreed to let him use it. My bike was my pride and joy, but he needed it to complete his Goth appearance. Fortunately, he knew how to ride a bike.

As the vamps got into their baby blue Mustang, Jack took a minute to fiddle with his phone. Mine zinged with a message from him. He stuck the phone under the seat, got on the bike and started up the engine. I had to make sure he was careful with my bike before I read his text.

We are going to the Sports Bar on Magnolia Road.

When the vamps and Jack were gone from the parking lot, Pete started the truck. "Where to?"

I showed him the text, and within minutes, we were headed back to Denham Springs. About thirty minutes later, we pulled up into the parking lot of our destination. Despite the sign that read KARAOKE NIGHT, the place only had a few patrons.

Sad. I so wanted to hear a bunch of drunks sing off key.

My bike and the Mustang were parked off in the far end of the parking lot, and as there wasn't any sign of Jack or the vamps, they had to be already inside.

The three of us got out of the truck and entered the bar as inconspicuously as possible. An old man stood on the stage singing a country pop song about a teenage girl whining over her lost love. I raised my eyebrow.

At least with a bunch of drunks there'd be a variety of terrible singing. Tonight, ladies and gentlemen, we are stuck with the same voice over and over. Oh joy.

Pete led the way to a booth in the darkest corner of the bar, and after taking notice of where Jack and his companions sat, I took the seat with my back to them. Pete and Kate slid into the other side, and he immediately draped his arm over her shoulder.

The waitress took our orders and pretty much left us alone after that. We refrained from making small talk in order to hear the conversation between Jack and the vamps. Fortunately, they were quite loud, so I didn't need to exert any powers to listen in. I didn't worry about the twins smelling my angel blood as I had eaten a lot of garlic for lunch, which hid scents quite well from vampires.

"So, Jack," purred Marishka. "You like the dark side of life, too." There was a tremor of wickedness in her voice.

I'll show you some darkness. About six feet of it. I bit my lip to keep my butt in my seat. *Chill, Angelle. Flirting is part of the game, and Jack isn't yours.*

Jack was slow with his response, and I could tell he had weighed his words carefully. "You could say the dark holds a certain … fascination for me."

Her laughter was deep, like an imitation of an evil queen from a bad B movie. "You amuse me, Jack. You are …" She sniffed his skin. "Rare. I think I shall keep you for a while."

"Seeing as we just met, that's nice to know." Jack took a sip of his beer.

The country vamp leaned her head against his chest and patted it lightly. "Good, strong heartbeat. I like that in a man."

My eyes met Kate's, and we both nodded in unison. My words were soft. "Gotta be the scorned bride. Can't wait to stake her."

I took a sip of beer and realized I had missed some conversation.

"—only hungry for one thing," the country vamp purred.

"Do they have it here?" Jack asked, as if he didn't have a clue he was on the menu.

"Mmm-hmm."

Music from the jukebox filled my ears as Jack and the vamps lapsed into silence. The distinct sounds of sloppy kissing confirmed that Jack was her food of choice. I hoped he kept her from puncturing his skin.

"I want a taste," Marishka said.

"Sure, darling," Jack slurred. "You know what they say … two twins are better than one."

Our waitress brought our food and drinks, placing them haphazardly in front of us. She moved away, and the next half hour consisted of listening to the Karaoke singer warbled and stumbled over song after song. Jack and the twins made small talk, or rather, small smacks. I sort of hoped management would see the make-out session and kick them out. The twins apparently had that glamour thing going because nobody but me, Kate and

Pete noticed them. The waitress never returned to refill Jack's drink, either.

"Will this never end?" I sighed.

Kate reached across the table and patted my hand. "Easy, girl."

"Easy, my ass. They haven't talked in over twenty minutes. I'm surprised they haven't been thrown out due to indecent exposure of the tongue."

"Ooo, someone's jealous," Pete said in a sing song.

"Bite me." I resisted the urge to throw a fry at him.

Pete sat up and pulled some bills out of his wallet, dropping them on the table. "They're leaving."

We clamored to our feet and exited the bar in time to see the red taillights of the Mustang making a beeline out of the parking lot. My bike remained, and anger slammed into me.

"What the demon's wings? He can't just leave her there."

Kate and Pete began sneezing simultaneously. When it continued, I gave them a strange look before assessing the area around us. Next to the door laid the keys to my bike. Apparently, Jack had dropped them on his way out. The keys, however, were not what was making the Weres sneeze.

Scattered around the door were stems of purple flowers. To the ordinary human, they were pretty and fragrant and out of season. To the Weres, they stopped up their noses, and effectively threw them off the vamps scent.

A shiver raced down my spine. Where had they gone? Jack knew better than to try and handle two vamps on his own. I hoped he hadn't grossly underestimated those two and decided to play the Lone Hero.

I reached for my cell phone and sent him a text. It was useless to try to catch up with them. They were long gone by this point.

"Sorry," Kate sneezed and ran to the truck to get away from the poisonous purple wolfs bane.

"Meet me at the bar," I said to Pete as he hightailed it to the truck as well.

Glumly, I went over to my bike and opened the compartment under the seat. I froze at the sight of Jack's cell phone.

***

Scorned

CHAPTER 8

The Lusty Crow
Watson
Thursday, December 21st, 2:30 AM
Countdown: 11 Days 13 Hours 29 Minutes 59 Seconds

Sitting on a barstool, I stared at the door and twisted a lock of hair with my left hand. The hour was nearing two thirty a.m. and still no sign of Jack.

We had closed thirty minutes ago, and except for the front door, the place was locked up tight. Ben stood behind the bar while Pete and Kate were perched on stools. Unable to contain my nervous energy, I pushed away from the bar, went to each table and straightened the red and white checkered tablecloths.

"My sinuses have cleared up. I can try picking up the scent if you want." Kate chewed her nails, something she always did when she was worried.

"No," I said. "He's a big boy. Hopefully, he can handle himself."

The door flew open, and the object of our concern sauntered in as if he hadn't a care in Watson. Spotting me, Jack weaved his way through the tables and sat down at the one I was fixing. He had on a goofy grin, and his eyes were a bit glossy.

"You drove in this condition?" Ben threw a towel over his shoulder and poured a glass of water. He passed it to Kate, who put it in Jack's hands.

"Oh no," I whispered. "Did you let them bite you?"

Jack frowned and showed us his neck. "Nope."

I laid into him. "Where have you been? What happened to going back to my place, and why the hell didn't you wait for us?"

Jack tried to snap his fingers, but it didn't quite work out too well for him. "Oh, yeah … I knew there was something I was supposed to do."

"Are you drunk?" I checked his pupils. All was clear in the land of Jack.

"Nope."

"Then where'd you go?"

His face turned beat red, and he ducked his head. His words were muffled, but I heard him. "Parking."

My eyes grew wide, and my heart lurched in annoying pain. *Get a grip, Angelle. You don't own him, and you certainly aren't boyfriend and girlfriend.*

"You went parking with a vampire?" I asked.

He held up two fingers and shrugged. "Two, actually. Maybe I misjudged them creatures of the night. They sure know how to make the dark interesting."

Bile rose, and my chest constricted with anger and jealousy. Even though I wanted Jack to learn some vampires were good, these weren't. "Jack, vampires killed your mother, remember?"

He stared at me as the memory returned, and the carefree light faded from his eyes. I hated doing that as God knew it was hard to be lighthearted these days, but these vamps were dangerous.

"These girls aren't evil," he argued. "They didn't kill; didn't drain my blood. We had a good time. That's all. Why do you have to turn it in to something ugly?"

I was shocked at his odd behavior, but I had to know the truth. "Are you still on our team?"

Jack scoffed. "Of course I am."

The others had remained quiet, but Pete spoke up. "Well, did you find anything out? Do you think they're part of the riddle?"

Jack made a face and shook his head. "Nope."

An air of defeat settled over everyone, but I still had my suspicions about those two vamps. I wanted to pick his brains dry of information, but he slowly got to his feet.

"I gotta use the bathroom. I'll be right back." He left the room, and we all looked blankly at each other.

I was dumbfounded. "He's been bit. Maybe not on the neck, but he's been bit somewhere."

I made the mistake of looking at Ben, who had a silly grin on his face. I shook my finger at him. "Don't even go there."

He held up his hands. "Hey, it's possible."

"He's got a point," Kate said. "His penis would be the perfect area to hide a bite mark."

A mental image of those twins sucking on his handsome face popped in my head. I got other visuals, and I tossed the napkin I'd been folding down on the table. Jack sauntered out of the restroom.

"Spill it, Jack. How far did you go?" I demanded.

His brows pulled slightly upward, and he held up his hands. "I swear it was just kissing.

Nobody spoke. We just looked at him.

His baby blues stared into my eyes. "I swear. You can inspect me if you want."

My mouth watered, and my blood tingled with anticipation. I could hear my little hormones going 'yes, yes, and yes'. Did I dare? "Full body?"

He nodded. "Whatever it takes to set your mind at ease."

My mind might be put at ease, but the rest of my body … The thought of seeing him naked had me paralyzed with lust. I swallowed and absentmindedly began folding the napkin again

Ben cleared his throat. "She can't."

"I can," Kate piped up.

"Hey," Pete objected.

She patted his knee. "It's just an inspection."

Jack stared intently at me, and I swallowed over the sudden dryness in my throat. I pointed at my office. "Kate and I will check you over in there."

"Said the spider to the fly," Jack whispered.

I led the way and held the door for Kate and Jack, and then I entered and locked the door. Pressing my back against the door, I stared at Jack. He stood the middle of the room, and pulled his shirt up and over his head before tossing it on the floor. In less than a minute, he was down to his briefs. The thin material revealed how turned on he was, and I threw my hand out as his thumb hooked in the waistband. I swallowed so I wouldn't drool all over myself.

"Whoa. No need to rush. I'm distracted enough as it is," I said.

Jack waited in all his lusciousness. I pinched myself to make sure I wasn't dreaming. Besides, shouldn't I still be mad at him for parking with those vamps? The thought sobered me up and gave me the strength to get close to him without jumping his boner ... uh, bones.

"I've got his front," Kate said with a little too much excitement in her voice.

I stepped behind him, and once it was obvious his back was clear of any vampire bites, I started checking out his legs. My mouth watered. There was something delicious about a well-muscled, curly haired male leg.

My hands had a mind of their own. I started with his left ankle, and my hands ate up his flesh. His calf was thick and firm, and I caressed the underside of his knee ... all in the name of checking him out for bites, of course. His thighs spoke of hidden power, and I stopped where flesh met briefs. I took my time with the other leg, thoroughly enjoying myself. It was a miracle I didn't turn into a pile of mashed potatoes. I was so not headed down the right path to salvation right now.

A low moan slipped out of Jack's mouth, but I couldn't tell if it was a reaction from my touch or Kate's. She backed off immediately.

"No bites up front. How about the back?"

Standing, I backed away and sat on the edge of the couch. "Nothing."

I stared at his beautifully shaped behind. He turned around and stared down at me. I couldn't speak, couldn't move.

Kate tapped Jack on the shoulder. "Drop the briefs, stud."

He faced her and did as she asked. I admired the nice view of his bared behind, grateful I didn't have the temptation of inspecting the other side of his luscious body. It didn't take her long to confirm the rest of him bite-free. Jack put his clothes back on.

"So did you and the vamps do any talking?" I asked. "Or was it just a mack session?"

He shrugged. "We didn't talk much."

I bit back jealousy. "Okay. Do you remember where you … parked?" The word felt bitter and foreign on my tongue.

"Yeah, but it wasn't anywhere special. Kinda close to the road. I think it led to the gravel pits, but it was blocked off."

"Probably the same driveway I followed them to the other night." I picked lint off my pants.

Kate headed toward the door. "Well, I'm tired, and I'm going home."

Jack smiled at me. "Am I free to leave?"

I pulled his cell phone out of my back pocket and tossed it to him. "Yep."

"Ok. See you tomorrow." He left my office whistling.

What the hell just happened to the man who hated vampires with a passion?

***

Scorned

The Lusty Crow
Watson, LA
Thursday, December 21ˢᵗ, 10:00 p.m.
Countdown: 10 Days 17 Hours 59 Minutes 59 Seconds

Exhaustion helped me sleep through the morning and early afternoon. The minute I woke, however, the riddle popped in my head. I fretted until I got the text from Ben asking for help at the bar because two waitresses had called in sick. I was grateful for the opportunity to do something, and a few hours passed while I served drinks and food. Pete and Jack had even showed up to help in the kitchen. I wanted to question him about his erratic behavior, but there hadn't been time. Yet again, I had to fill in for a sick waitress.

I leaned against the bar, waiting on Ben to get me a round of drinks for some customers. The door opened, and a tiny woman with dull brown hair walked in. She reminded me of a mouse with her upturned nose and dark brown eyes.

She reeked of vampire, but her blood still smelled human. The little mouse took a seat at the other end of the bar, and I fine-tuned my hearing as Ben went to get her order - a diet coke and bourbon. On the way back down to my end of the bar, his puppy-brown eyes met mine in mutual understanding. He knew something was odd about her as well.

I went about my business but kept an eye on Miss Mouse. She stayed low key, avoiding everyone that entered and stared into her drink. Most everyone failed to notice her, and the more they did, the more fidgety she became. I was thankful she wasn't wearing a trench coat, or I'd have to watch for any concealed weapons. I certainly didn't want some crazy lunatic pulling out a gun and shooting up my bar because she had a problem.

A lone biker came in and sat two barstools down from her. I became distracted by some customers making small talk, and when I checked on Miss Mouse, Biker Boy had moved to the stool right beside her. They seemed to hit it off, and even though everything appeared normal, something didn't feel right.

"What do you think?" I asked Ben.

"Smells vampy, but she's not. Strange. Must be under the spell of one."

"Maybe she's acting as bait," I suggested. "Luring the guy back to meet his death."

Taking a seat on a stool, I kept an eye on Miss Mouse and Biker Boy. I eavesdropped but unfortunately, Miss Mouse and Biker Boy only made idle, get-to-know-ya chit-chat. She did talk a lot about her ex-boyfriend, and I got the impression she was a woman scorned.

Ben leaned on the bar. "I know that look."

Focusing on him, I kept my voice low. "Something's not right with the woman. I don't trust her. She needs to be followed."

I looked around. There were only two other couples in the place besides Miss Mouse and Biker Boy. "Hopefully, they'll be our last customers, and I can tail them."

Ben frowned at me. "You just want to skip out on the cleaning."

While true, I simply smiled. "Gotta love me."

"Actually, I don't gotta … but I do anyway." He sprayed down the bar with cleaner.

I watched the last few patrons leave except my prey. So while they continued getting to know each other, I started cleaning. I even stacked the chairs on the tables, hoping they'd get the hint.

They didn't. Typically, the bar stayed open as long as customers paid. So, I re-took my stool and stuck my nose in a paper.

"Glad to see you didn't skip out on cleaning," Ben said as he put a glass of water in front of me.

"Ha ... ha."

A half hour later, Miss Mouse and Biker Boy left. I nodded at Ben and turned to slip out of the back door, but Kate burst out of my office before I took two steps.

She gasped. "The fan's about to spit caca." It was obvious she'd been running from something, and with anxiety in her green eyes, she surveyed the room.

"Why?"

"Two vampires stumbled upon me as I was hunting in the woods across the street. I took off running south, jumped across Highway 16 and circled around to slip in through your back door. But I don't think I lost them."

"Why do you think they are chasing you?" My angel-sense tingled up and down my spine.

"Probably because I took their meal with me," Kate replied.

She stepped to my left to reveal a wide-eyed, frightened little girl who was holding a teddy bear and wearing a nightgown. She sucked her thumb like it was ice cream, and I went into panic mode.

"Lock her in my office and make double – no, triple sure the back door is locked." I looked at Ben. "Lock the front door. Pete! Jack! We've got company coming!"

The two men burst through the kitchen door. Both wore aprons that had "Kiss this cook ... and you're toast" on them.

I managed a half smile. "Lost at cards with Dirk, eh?"

They both wrestled to get the aprons off and tossed them back into the kitchen. Ben threw us each a couple sharp stakes from behind the bar before obeying my previous order. He took two steps toward the entrance, but he was too late.

No less than eight vampires sauntered into my bar. Two were women.

"We're closed," I stated.

The leader sneered at me. "That so? Well, we'll leave once the bitch gives us back our meal."

I glanced at Kate as she stood guard in front of my office where she'd stowed the little girl. I playfully balanced the wooden stake between my hands.

"That's so not gonna happen."

"I figured you'd say that, so you're going to take the little girl's place." He crossed his arms while the female behind him draped her arms possessively around him. She rested her chin on his shoulder, and her long bleach-blonde hair fell over his chest. Dark sunglasses hid the color of her eyes, and she stretched out her fingers across his chest. The blood-red polish on her one inch nails splashed in contrast against his plaid shirt.

This guy was a real winner. He looked like he'd just stepped off the farm with faded blue-jeans and an LSU baseball hat. The rest of his vamp-gang wore the same type of country clothing that fit snugly to their well-toned, athletic bodies.

My hair brushed my shoulders as I shook my head. "See, I have a little problem with your plan. I kind of enjoy not being dead."

"Then, I sure hope you have insurance on this place, lady," he growled.

I twirled the stake in my right hand and took a fighting stance. I smiled sweetly. "Let's just say they're like a good neighbor."

The female disengaged herself from the leader's body and stepped in front of him. She placed her hand on her hip, and her long, blood-red fingernails tapped against her tight jeans. "Think you're pretty tough with that stake, dontcha, sweetie?"

I sighed, already bored. Same old stereotypical vampire, same old fight. Why oh why did these new age vampires watch so many movies? If I still had celestial wings, I'd give a few feathers to Nate for a chance to take out an old vamp, but they were smart. They kept hidden and let these young fools keep hunters like myself occupied.

"Let me knock those sunglasses off your face." I stood my ground, refusing to throw the first punch.

Out of the corner of my eye, I saw Pete jump over the half wall separating the eating area from the dance floor. Jack whizzed past as well, but as the female closed the space between us, my full attention was focused on her rather than the other small fights sprouting up around the bar.

"I'd like to see you try," she purred and swung her hand at my face. I pulled back, but the tips of her fingernails grazed my right cheek. The minor scratch was easy to ignore as I counter-attacked.

I jabbed my left fist into her chin, and the sunglasses popped off her face like a cap off a beer bottle. She staggered back with wide eyes.

My mouth lifted in a half-smile. "Surprise surprise."

"Bitch," she snarled and lunged at me.

Big mistake. Her chest met my stake, and she exploded into dust. Her remains floated in the air, and through them, I saw her man glowering at me. He lunged, and I met him head on.

With hands the size of a paperback book, he grabbed me around the throat and lifted me in the air. I ignored the sudden lack of oxygen and landed a powerful kick to his groin. He dropped me on my butt. I sprang to my feet and attacked while he rolled around on the ground.

My stake met his heart, and I sent him to Hell as quick as I had sent his girlfriend.

I stood up and surveyed the room. Ben stood on the half-wall holding the head of the vampire he had been fighting. The body had just turned to dust, and the head was the last to ash-out. Ben met my eyes and grinned. At least someone was enjoying himself.

I looked at the dance floor just as Pete took out another vamp. The wolf's back was to me, and the vampire dust settled over him.

My gaze went past him to watch as Jack lifted a vamp in the air with one hand. My blood ran cold. No mere human could lift a six foot eight, heavily muscled vamp and toss him against the wall like a rag doll. Jack slammed his fist into the vamp's chest, and another one bit the dust.

My heart throbbed with pain, and my stomach twisted in on itself. There was no doubt in my mind now. Jack was a blood addict.

***

CHAPTER 9

The Lusty Crow
Watson, LA
Friday, December 22nd, 3:00 AM
Countdown: 10 Days 12 Hours 59 Minutes 59 Seconds

"Okay, who isn't dead?" I asked.

Twirling the stake in my right hand, I looked around the room, hoping I could take out one more. A thin layer of annihilated vampires dust covered the entire bar. Jack stood on the stage with his shirt ripped from one shoulder to the waist, and his bare, sweaty chest beckoned for my fingers. I could even see the trail of sexy hair leading into the front of his butt-hugging jeans.

Blood addict.

Those two little words chased off the lustful thoughts. When a human drank from a vampire without being bitten, they become a blood addict and are controlled by the vamp. The addict would do whatever their master asked of them. The up-side was the increased strength and longevity of life. The down-side … without a vampire's blood, the human would die. That thought alone chased off the lust-bugs threatening me.

"Angelle," Kate called from behind me.

I turned to the dance area. Pete lay on the floor with his legs and arms sprawled out at odd angles. A silver knife stuck out of his chest. Ben knelt over him. Fear rose in my chest and momentarily cut off my breath.

When I got to them, Ben whispered, "Do you want to know who's un-dead or just not dead?"

I shook my head and wrinkled my nose at him before kneeling beside Pete. "Kate, do you still have your grandmother's special ointment?"

Tears slipped out of the corners of Kate's green eyes. She placed her fingers on the knife's handle, and her skin hissed and smoked. Snatching her hand to her chest, she said, "That's pure silver. This is bad."

"Come on, girl, get it together," I snapped. My fingers wrapped around the hilt of the knife and pulled it out. Blood gushed out of the wound, but it wasn't deep. The silver had taken him down, not the blade.

"Is he a Werewolf?" Jack's voice boomed behind me, loud enough for the dead to hear.

"Ben, get him to Kate's grandmother," I ordered.

The vampire picked up the unconscious Werewolf and hurried out of the bar with Kate on his heels. Standing up, I faced Jack.

"Would you kill him if I said yes?"

His glaring blue eyes burned a hole in my forehead. "He just saved me from a vamp. I'm not a complete idiot, Angelle, and I really wish you would quit treating me like one."

He advanced on me and I backed up until my legs hit the stage.

"What are you doing?" I asked. We were alone, but from the look in his eyes, I don't think that would have mattered.

In answer, his hot body pressed into me, and his hands seized my shoulders. He kissed my forehead and led a trail of fire down my nose to my chin.

Tilting my head back, he licked from my chin to in between my breasts. My heart was pounding, and my bra felt too tight. I shoved him back.

"I can't."

"Why not? You know you want to." He growled and took a step toward me. "Sex is best after the heat of battle."

He took one more step, and I scrambled onto the stage.

"Back off, Jack. I mean it."

"No."

"I thought you understood. In order to get into Heaven, I can't have extramarital sex."

He jumped onto the stage from a standing position. His sexually feral approach reminded me of a lion. I took a step back each time he stepped closer. I knew I needed to run, but his hungry gaze held me prisoner.

He pressed me against the wall, placed each of his hands on either side of me and licked his lips. "I want to taste your mouth."

My heart fluttered like a little bird with a broken wing. I couldn't resist him. His kiss took my soul away, and I gave it to him willingly. Thank God Jack wasn't the devil, or I'd be in deep trouble.

Jack's tongue played with the corner of my mouth. He teased the inside of my lip before mating with my tongue. I sighed and closed my eyes, thoroughly enjoying my decent into temptation.

He tapped my temple with his finger, and my eyes popped open. His hypnotic blue eyes were dilated with desire, and lust sang in my own blood.

Setting my mouth free, he pressed a feathery kiss on every inch of my face. I shivered as he attacked my neck. His teeth nipped my skin. I tilted my head to the right, allowing him easier access.

His exposed neck beckoned for a taste. I wanted to run my tongue over it and taste its saltiness. It drove me near mad, and my lips ached.

Jack pressed his lower body against mine, and I shivered and pushed him back … or rather, tried to. I pushed again, thinking I hadn't tried hard enough. Wrong. When he didn't budge this time, I panicked and used every ounce of strength I had on him. It should have sent him flying across the room. Instead, he only stumbled back a few steps. My mouth went instantly dry, and fear settled in my stomach.

"That's not right." I didn't want to say out loud that I thought he was a blood addict. I kept seeing the image of Jack throwing the male vamp into the wall before staking him.

"What?" He smiled as if he knew a secret I didn't.

"You're stronger than me." My hands shook.

"Really? I hadn't noticed."

Jack took a step closer, and I placed my hand on his chest to stop him. His skin felt good beneath my fingers, and I shook my head clear of desire.

"I want to do this with you, Jack," I whispered. My voice became trapped in my throat, making it husky. "But we can't."

Disappointment clouded his face. "You're being a tease, Angelle."

"Yeah? Well, if I am, it's because you're making me. Stop stealing kisses …"

He swooped in and took possession of my mouth again. I sank into his spell. *What harm can be done? It's just a kiss.*

'A kiss can lead a man to acts of wild abandonment.' Cal's voice filled my head.

The words helped, and I pulled back. Unfortunately, Jack was still lost to desire, but he seemed to have gotten back his common sense. He leaned his forehead against mine. "Okay. We'll take this slow."

"Thank you."

"I better go." Backing up a few steps, he stood with one hand on his hip and the other scratching his head as if undecided about leaving.

"I like you, Ange. I like you more than just a kissing buddy." He crossed his arms. "This is a good thing happening between us, and I don't want to screw it up, so let's call it a night."

I raised my left eyebrow, surprised at his admission. Apparently, he had given some thought to us having some sort of relationship. *Interesting ...*

"Well, that sounds like a good idea to me," I replied.

Jack jumped down from the stage and held his hands out to help me. I could have easily gotten down, but I let his chivalrous side have his way. I braced my hands on his shoulders, and his hands slid up my sides and under my arms. He lifted me up like I was a leaf and set me gently down.

"Thanks," I mumbled, a tad disconcerted. Obviously, I had to get a better handle on thwarting the lust between us. It could get out of hand real quick, and I'd lose my ticket into Heaven.

He let go of me and took a step toward the door. A piercing scream filled the building and sent my heart into my throat. The scream came from my office.

What the demon-wings was going on?

***

The Lusty Crow
Watson, LA
Friday, December 22nd, 3:30 AM
Countdown: 10 Days 12 Hours 29 Minutes 59 Seconds

I held the stake in my right hand and over my head, prepared to dust any vampire that dared take up residence in my office. Jack stood behind me, wielding a knife. Placing my left hand on the doorknob, I took a deep breath. I didn't have a clue what to expect, but when I pushed open the door, what we found did not even meet *those* lack of expectations.

The little girl sat on the desk with her legs hanging over the side. She leaned back on her hands, and her head was thrown back as she continued screaming. Her teddy bear hugged her neck, and upon our entrance, the now-animated stuffed toy lifted its head and looked at us.

"What the hell is that?" Jack asked.

Blood dripped from the bear's pointed teeth, and the brown eyes swirled with demonic green. Sliding away from the little girl, the twelve inch tall teddy bear balanced on the edge of the desk in a karate stance. Two inch long claws grew out of its paws.

"Um, Teddy Kruger?" I suggested. "And I'm guessing he lives on Elm Street."

The nightmarish bear sprung into the air, did a double flip and rammed its plush feet into my chest. The force pushed me back a step or two, but I remained on my feet. When the bear landed and saw I wasn't flat on my butt, his mouth moved as if saying a curse word, but, alas, he had no vocal chords to actually spew the offending verbiage. Apparently, Teddy thought he was dealing with a normal human. I was glad to show him wrong.

Teddy bared his plush fangs and issued a growl meant to rattle the bones of the dead. Unfortunately, the growl equaled the volume of a newborn kitten growling.

I raised my left eyebrow. "Seriously? That's your scary? If you wanted to impress me, you should have possessed something with a little more fear factor."

With a mini-roar, the demon-possessed bear raised its tiny paws, and green electricity zapped from its razor sharp claws. I jumped to the left and into Jack. His hands grasped my arms and helped steady me. The electricity slammed into the wall beside us. A black scorch mark the size of a bowling ball obliterated the paint.

The teddy bear climbed onto the coffee table, picked up a ceramic coaster and hurled it at me. I caught it and threw it right back at the bear, smacking it right in the forehead. The demonic-plush toy fell onto its back, and while it lay stunned, I rushed over and pinned it to the coffee table with my left hand.

"Why are you attacking this little girl? Aren't there tastier meals?" I asked.

The bear's mouth moved, but again, nothing came out. Its eyes narrowed, and it looked at its right paw. Using its left paw, it pushed against the red heart sticker in the middle of the right paw.

"I love you," said a sweet gushy voice from the teddy bear's sound box.

I laughed. "Well the feeling isn't mutual."

The bear frowned and pressed again. "I need a hug."

This time, Jack laughed. "I don't suppose there are any curse words programmed in that computer chip."

Growling, the bear sank its two inch claws down my forearms. Pain hit me like a tidal wave. Blood gushed from the wounds, and I let go of the bear. The pain subsided quickly, but I knew the energy from my blood would help the demon stay in the stuffed animal. The bear didn't even have to drink the blood – just let it soak over and into him.

The bear lunged at me, and I jabbed the stake into its plush stomach. White cotton gushed out like guts, and green electricity surged out of its eyes, over its body and exploded in a cloud. No longer animated, the bear sank to the coffee table. Its plush arms and legs twisted in a heap. More cotton spilled out, along with a wooden key whose top was shaped like an owl. I scooped up the key, turning it over to find a strange inscription on the back: I3413.

The little girl stopped screaming, and her body shook as green electricity shimmered over her. Her legs became longer, and her body morphed into a female fallen angel. She wore a pink, frilly dress, and her hair was dyed pink. Her black wings stretched out as she slid lithely off the desk.

"Hey, Angie," said the bubble gum smacking fallen angel. "Thanks for releasing me from that spell."

Lifting my left eyebrow, I crossed my arms and tilted my head back. "Well if it isn't Nate's current flavor of Hades."

"What the hell is she?" Jack stammered.

"Ooo, who is that luscious human behind you?" asked the fallen angel. She batted her long lashes at him and tried to step around me.

I blocked her path and held up my hand, using the owl-shaped key as a pointer. "Back off, Tabitha. He's off limits."

She closed her eyes and inhaled deeply. Pouting, she looked back at me. "He smells funny anyway."

Faster than I could even see, Tabitha grabbed the wooden key from my hand and moved across the room. "Thanks again for releasing me from those vamps spell. You know how much they love angel blood, even if it is of the dark variety."

I took a step toward her, but she pulled out a yellow, green and red gun. Sneering, I took another step. "Really? A water gun?"

Tabitha squeezed the trigger, and I jumped back and into Jack, dodging what I thought was a bullet. It was not.

A thin black rope quickly slipped over my ankles and wound around the rest of my body like a python. The rope ensnared Jack as well, pinning our bodies tightly together. We fell to the floor in a tangle of arms and legs. I struggled but quickly realized my strength was contained as surely as my legs and arms. I ceased fighting.

A pair of pink stilettos appeared before me, and I looked up at the fallen angel. "Let us go," I growled.

Tabitha blew a large pink bubble. "Ha. Right."

She held up the key and slipped it into her bra and winked. "Thanks for getting this back for me. Nate would flay me alive if I'd lost this. Enjoy that lust demon riding on your shoulder."

A black cloud enveloped her, and she disappeared in it. Eventually, it cleared, and I realized that Jack and I were spooning. His hot breath fanned my neck, and his arms encircled me with his hands nestled underneath my breasts. Heat pooled through my body, and I cursed.

Not only had Tabitha taken off with what I was certain was a clue to the riddle, but she'd also effectively ensnared me in a trap meant to tempt and test my vow of virtue. The lust demon she referred to raised its sinful head and immediately began playing with my hormones.

Heaven help me ...

***

CHAPTER 10

The Lusty Crow
Watson, LA
Friday, December 22ⁿᵈ, 6:00 AM
Countdown: 10 Days 9 Hours 59 Minutes 59 Seconds

"Would you please stop squirming?" I snapped.
"We've already established that this rope is magically enhanced and unbreakable."

"Actually, I'm quite comfortable," Jack whispered against the back of my neck. "But your hair keeps getting in my mouth, and I'm trying to move some of it out of the way."

My hands rested on top of his muscular arm, and I absently played with the light spraying of hair on his arm. "Sorry."

"Will the magic wear off?"

"Highly unlikely." I glanced at the clock on the wall above the one-way window. "And I don't foresee anybody getting here anytime soon. The restaurant opens at eleven, so the staff will get here about ten. That gives us four hours of quality bonding time."

"Bondage time so soon? But we just met."

"Ha ha."

Jack and I lay on our left side, and he tried to shift his left arm. "Sorry, it's falling asleep."

The clock's ticking beat against my ears. An eighteen wheeler's engine roared as it drove past the bar, and another truck laid down on its horn. I wished we had an early morning delivery scheduled for today, but we didn't. The trucks were just part of the everyday traffic.

Jack's light snoring tickled my ear, and my mouth fell open. Seriously? How on earth could he even think about sleeping right now? *Men.*

I replayed the events of the night, wondering how the owl key and Tabitha fit into the riddle. That fallen angel oversaw the nightlight demons, hence her little girl outfit. Those demons terrorized kids. As far as I could figure from the clues received so far, kids were not part of the equation, but I could be wrong. The only thing I was certain of was that I had to get that key back.

Jack moved his fingers, and they brushed the underside of my breast. I narrowed my eyes and wiggled. "Nice to see you're awake. Cut it out."

He laughed. "Not much I can do to avoid them in the position we are in."

"That's a feeble excuse."

Jack yawned. "Too bad we can't turn on the TV."

"You could go back to sleep and snore in my ear again."

He tried to move, but our bodies only seemed to meld together even more. I tried not to think of how good Jack's body felt against mine, but the more I fought the thoughts, the more they plagued me.

"I tried to raise my mother from the grave," Jack whispered.

My jaw dropped. *Wow, that came out of the clear sky.* "Seriously?"

"Yeah," he drawled.

"You're a necromancer?"

Jack snorted. "Not even close."

"Details please."

He sighed, his breath warming the back of my neck. "It was three months after my parents were buried. It was midnight, and the cemetery was empty. I put candles around her grave and spread the chicken's blood over it and on my face. By the way, blood really stinks, y'know."

I did know, but he was freaked out enough by non-humans that I refrained from agreeing with him.

"Well, I said the words and did the dance, but the earth remained solid over my mother's grave."

"Where'd you get the ritual from?" I asked warily.

"Some voodoo shop in New Orleans," he admitted. "It was not one of my finer moments. And then to end the perfect night, Dusty showed up. I can still hear his laughter."

His story tugged at my heart strings. "You were still a boy who needed his mother. Nothing stupid about that. Grief makes us do crazy things."

The ticking clock had become annoying. Every time we lapsed into silence, the ticks seemed to become louder and louder. It reminded me that we had a riddle to solve.

"There was an inscription on the back of that key Tabitha took," I said. "I hate to say this, but I have to get it back from her."

"So it's a clue?"

"I'm not positive, but I think so."

"What was the inscription?"

"I3413."

The screen on the television flickered, and my heart jumped in my throat. Swallowing over the fear in my mouth, I whispered, "Did you see that?"

"Yeah."

The screen lit up, and an image of a female vampire filled the screen. Haughtily, she tossed her head back and sneered at me. The tip of her fang slid down and pierced her lower lip. A drop of blood pooled but did not continue down. Instead, it followed her mouth to the corner where it hit her skin and branched off into several different directions at once, like a massive red firework display.

The right side of the vampire's face resembled a spider web made of red silk. The blood touched her eye and exploded, leaving a bloody, gaping hole.

I closed my eyes, but when I reopened them, she was still there. Only now, the hair on the right side of her head was gone and patches of skull showed through the blistered skin. Gray matter seeped through those wounds as if her brain were being pushed out of her head.

I narrowed my eyes. Did the broadcaster of this message think this would scare me? If so, they didn't know me at all. It would take more than a little visual graphics for someone who had lived through horrors made of touch, smell and taste.

Nate had educated me well. I wondered if he would have taken me with him had he known he was training me to fight against his very own demon army. God probably knew, which is why He had let me go with His nemesis.

"That was gross," Jack whispered.

The TV screen returned to black. "Is it just me, or did that look like one of those vampire twins?"

Jack snorted. "That hag looked nothing like Marishka."

I frowned. The vampire I had seen was gorgeous with shiny black hair and porcelain skin. Well, she was pretty before her face cracked up. "Just so we're clear … what did she look like to you?"

"Old wrinkled face … scraggly gray hair. Huge wart on her nose."

Actually, this was great news. It meant that the twins were trying to scare me away, and the fact that they hid their true image from Jack assured me that whether or not he was a blood addict, he was still under their spell. Of course, that was the bad news.

***

The Lusty Crow
Watson, LA
Friday, December 22nd, 10:00 AM
Countdown: 10 Days 5 Hours 59 Minutes 59 Seconds

"Well, don't you two look cozy."

My eyes popped opened, and I looked at the door. Ben stood with his hand on the knob and sported a silly grin.

"There's an explanation," I mumbled. Blinking the sleep from my eyes, I couldn't believe I had fallen asleep. "Can you cut us lose?"

Ben nodded. "I'll get a knife from the kitchen. Stupid magic-enhanced ropes. "

"Get a zip lock bag too," I said.

A few seconds later, he knelt beside us and sliced through the rope. Jack helped me up.

"I have to go to Hell," I said while stretching my arms to get the kinks out.

"For what?" Ben asked.

"Tabitha did this to us, and she has a clue to the riddle." I gave him a run-down of the demonic bear fight and how the little girl had been a fallen angel caught in a spell. "She took off with a key that had an inscription on it: I3413. I don't suppose you know what that means?"

Ben scratched his head in thought. "No."

Kneeling by the spot where Tabitha had stood, I scooped the black ash into the bag. The ash was part of her essence. Only fallen angels left this when they moved between realms. Usually, the ash disappeared within a few hours. As such, Tabitha's ash only amounted to a tablespoon.

"What are you gonna do with that?" Jack asked.

"Use it to track her when I get there."

I locked the bag and looked at Ben. "Keep an eye on things while I'm gone."

"Wait," Jack put his hand on my wrist. "You're really going to Hell? How?"

"The demon who cursed me can get me there." I pulled my arm from his grasp, went to the cabinet on the other side of the desk and pulled out a ten inch curved blade. I tucked it into my boot and stuffed into my pockets a handful of red cherry bombs the size of grapes. The last items I grabbed were two jewelry-sized satchels, which I hung around my neck. The contents of the black one would get me home, and the blue satchel held celestial angel ash, which I had gotten from the kitchen angel who lived at my place.

Ben blocked my path. "Don't do this."

"Move please. Tabitha's ash is disappearing as we speak. I have to go now."

Ben narrowed his eyes but reluctantly stepped aside. I hurried into the ladies' bathroom and locked the door behind me. Turning off the lights, I faced the mirror.

I had fibbed about Robert, the demon, getting me into Hell. For this trip, I needed an escort who could protect me, and Bloody Mary owed me a favor.

Chanting her name, I sprinkled some of the celestial angel ash along the bottom of the mirror. The outline of a woman's upper torso appeared in the mirror, becoming more defined as I repeated her name. Her black hair held clumps of blood, and streaks of it covered her face. She held a toothbrush to her mouth, and when she saw me, she lowered it. Toothpaste foam covered her sharp teeth, and she smiled at me.

"Well, look who it is. My old battle buddy."

"Hey, Mary."

She spit and rinsed her mouth, dabbing her pale lips with a black towel. She applied blood-red lipstick. "So what can I do for ya?"

"I'm calling in that favor you owe me. I need to find someone in the Nightlight Kingdom."

Mary didn't need to know who just yet. That information might put her in a tight spot, seeing as how Tabitha was technically her boss.

The demon touched her one inch long fingernail to the glass and pushed through it. Her bony hand clawed its way into this realm and stuck out of the mirror with the palm up. My right hand reached to grasp her hand, and as our skin neared, my flesh crawled. I ignored the natural reaction, forcing myself to grab hold of her hand.

She yanked, and I closed my eyes, hating the feel of death as my body slid from the earth realm to Hell. My bodily functions shut down for one second. My heart stopped beating, and my lungs seemed to freeze. Ice filled my veins as death suffocated my being.

Just as quickly, everything started working again, and when I opened my eyes, I stood next to Bloody Mary. In this realm, she looked like an actress in a bad makeup job. In fact, the blood was actually strawberry jelly.

"Welcome back," she said.

"Not for long if I can help it."

Her hand now felt warm, and I let go of it and surveyed the bathroom. Four sinks lined the wall behind me, and four toilet stalls were in front of me. Cigarette smoke clogged the air and mixed with musky perfume.

"So you're teaching today?" I asked. "This is Demon High?"

"I'm the vice principal now," Mary said. "Got a promotion about five years ago."

"Nice," I drawled. "So someone else is teaching the new monsters how to scare, eh?"

"Yep."

I checked the stalls to ensure they were empty. "Can you keep me safe while I'm here?"

Mary's bloodshot eyes narrowed. "For how long?"

Holding up the bag of ashes, I shook them. "Long enough to find this bitch. She took something I need."

The demoness glanced at her watch. "If you can find her in thirty minutes, I'm your body guard. After that, I have a staff meeting."

"Cool." I opened the bag of ashes and dusted the air with them. They swirled like a mini-tornado, glided across the room and passed through the door like butter. We followed the dark floating mass as it traveled through the halls of the school and out the front doors.

We raced down the red sidewalks, past the black bushes with red flowers and across the red grass. Nate liked red and black, hence everything in Hell was a variation of those colors. He hated white, as it represented all things good. My skin had turned pink just from being there.

Tabitha's ash led us into the staff parking lot. The floating mass zipped up and over cars until it hovered over a bright red mini-van. Just as Mary and I stepped up to the sliding door, the ash sank through the roof, and Tabitha let out a blood-curling scream. I opened the door. The ash sat on top of her head. The soot formed daggers that had pierced her skull as it sank back into her head.

The fallen angel sat in the middle seat with a plate of food on her lap. When her meal meowed, my blood boiled. I grabbed the kitten from the pile of lettuce. Poor little thing trembled, but I didn't have time to undo the strings that bound her little legs together. I handed the little feline to Mary before pulling Tabitha out by her pigtails.

Fortunately, the fallen angel was stunned by the absorption of her ash into her body. I used that to my advantage and tossed her onto the nearest vehicle. She crumbled against the hood, and I pulled out the celestial angel ash and tossed it above her. The purple and pink glitter formed a net that settled over Tabitha, effectively pinning her to the hood of the car.

I approached her cautiously, and she sneered at me, showing her pointed teeth. "I'm gonna kick your ass when I get free, Angelle."

"No, you're not." I pointed to the kitten. "Does Nate know about this?"

Her eyes grew wide, and her lips trembled. I placed my hands on my hips and said, "From your reaction, I can see that he doesn't. So let's cut to the demon chase and come to an arrangement. I won't tell him you are snacking on his favorite pet, and you, in return, will give me that key AND stay away from me for the next … well, forever."

Tabitha swallowed and nodded. "Okay. I'll agree to that. The key's in the glove box."

I looked from her to the van, unease settling over me. Unfortunately, I didn't have time to be fearful. Every minute spent in Hell was an hour on earth. So far, I had been here eight minutes.

Sighing, I opened the passenger door and reached for the glove box. Mary's claw like fingers grabbed my hand. "Not a good idea. Let me."

She handed the kitten to me, and we swapped places. The second she opened the glove box, a black tarantula the size of a tea cup Yorkie dog jumped out and landed on Mary's chest. I shivered and jumped back, hugging the kitten. Mary grabbed the thing and held it away from her, making sure the three inch fangs were out of bite range. The spider was twice the size of a normal one.

"Ugh," I cringed, shutting my eyes. "That's your pet, Tabitha? Seriously?"

"Actually," Tabitha smirked. "It's Mary's. I was holding it for her."

When I looked at my old battle buddy, the spider had settled in the crook of her arm as she lovingly petted it. "Sorry, Angelle. I know you don't like spiders."

"That's putting it mildly." I closed my eyes as another wave of disgust hit me. "Can you get the key for me please?"

Mary dug in the glove box, pushing aside paper and junk. She pulled out the key and tossed it to me. "Debt settled."

I caught the key in my right hand and tucked it into my back pocket. The kitten fit snugly into my left hand. "Much appreciated. Later."

Leaving Bloody Mary and Tabitha in the staff parking lot, I raced back into the school just as the bell rang. A few teachers had gathered in the hall, and some appeared startled by my presence. One teacher stepped out of the classroom and froze when he saw me.

Rotten candy grew out of his bald head, and moldy candy corn replaced his ears. The Candyman rushed back into his classroom. He and I had fought long ago, and from the way his candy dropped, I knew he remembered the ass whipping I'd given him.

I continued running down the hall with the kitten. Just as I neared the bathroom, a clown came out of another classroom and blocked my path. I skidded to a halt as the clown's smile revealed a mouth full of razor sharp teeth. His colorful outfit defied Nate's red and black theme, and on the end of his hat was a ball that upon closer inspection turned out to be an eyeball.

"You have two choices," he said. "Stay and play … or run and die."

"Let's play." Reaching into my pocket, I pulled out one of the cherry bombs, popped the trigger and tossed it to him. He caught it out of reflex, and I dove to the ground as the bomb exploded, hugging the kitten to my chest. Bits of clown rained down as teenage monsters screamed and ran back into the classrooms.

Standing, I picked a large clump of clown from my hair. The gooey mess clung to my fingers. Cringing with disgust, I tossed it aside. I knew there was a reason I hated clowns.

"Well if it isn't my first true love," said a suave male voice from behind me.

My head snapped up as ice rolled down my spine. I turned to face the one person I never wanted to see again. I tucked the kitten under my left arm and placed my right hand on my hip. I gave him my best diva smile.

"Why, hello, Nate."

***

CHAPTER 11

Demon High School
Hell
Friday, December 22ⁿᵈ, 10:10 AM
Countdown: 10 Days 5 Hours 9 Minutes 59 Seconds

Nate stood with crossed arms and a stance that screamed *F with me and your soul is mine*. He wore a black tailored suit ironed to a crisp crease, and light reflected off his polished black shoes. He had a goatee and thin mustache, and his raven hair was parted on the side. Despite the look of softness, not a strand of his hair moved.

"My darling Angelle, I have missed you."

Uncrossing his arms, he slowly advanced on me. I backed up, trying to keep the direction going toward the bathroom. Escaping now would be high on my list of priorities.

"Can't say the feeling's mutual," I replied.

Before I could blink, Nate swooped in and pulled me into a hug. The kitten mewed in protest. His cologne took my breath away, enveloping me in a cloud. Lightheaded, I closed my eyes.

"So you come into my realm without paying homage to me?" His breath fanned my ear. "Do you remember what I do to trespassers?"

Long forgotten images flashed in my head, and I deeply wished I had escaped Demon High sooner. This was one trip down memory lane that I could've done without. The past played like a TV commercial in my head.

A human female from the 16th century crept down a darkened hallway. She was a witch and had used a spell to conjure up a portal to Hell. She headed toward a beacon of light that turned into a candelabra. It sat on a dining room table where Nate and a much younger version of myself resided. Food and goblets of various wine covered the table.

The female boldly approached. "I want immortality."

Nate slammed the goblet of wine on the table so hard the liquid sloshed over the sides. He tilted his head and studied the female. "And what shall ye give me for it?"

Her mouth dropped open. "I gave ye blood ... in the spell ... and ye revealed the portal."

His laugh bordered on cruelty. "The blood opened the portal, dear witch, not I."

He rose, and the chair screeched as he pushed it back. "Ye trespass."

The witch's eyes widened. "Nay."

"Pay homage to me."

She looked wildly about and grabbed a knife from the table, slicing her wrist. The skin remained intact, and no blood flowed.

Nate descended on her like a hawk on a mouse. He grabbed her by her shoulders. "Ye entered my realm without invitation ... and without a proper sacrifice. Perhaps I shall give ye what ye wish ... immortality."

He pushed her, and she fell back into an empty pit, screaming out when she hit the hard ground. Nate tossed a small sword into the pit, and the tip stuck in the dirt beside her. "Ye can use this to keep *slicing* for blood. Once ye give me a drop, then I'll set ye free to enjoy immortality."

The witch immediately pulled the knife out of the ground and drew the blade against her skin. She screamed as fire trailed in its wake. No blood pooled. She sliced time after time with the same result.

Nate slammed a hatch over the pit, and the scene blanked out.

I slowly opened my eyes, still in Nate's arms. "Oh, did I forget to pay homage to you? Sorry. Let me rectify that."

He let go of me, and I backed up. Reaching into my boot, I pulled out the ten inch curved sword he'd given that witch and slung it in his chest.

"Homage that."

Fire flamed in his chest from the tip of that sword. I'd saved the witch before I'd escaped Hell, and she'd given me the sword.

"And by the way," I smiled slowly. "Jeneen says hey."

Nate laughed wickedly as his body ignited in one huge flame. He held out his hands. "This won't kill me."

"I know."

The flame danced and caressed Nate. It ate up his clothes, singed his hair and charred his flesh. Yet through it all, his black eyes remained on me as if he were drinking in the sight of me. His cruel smile disappeared with his flesh, leaving a leering skeleton. Only his bones were black instead of white. His body exploded in smoke that trailed up into the ceiling.

"Dramatic much?" I whispered.

"To the end." Nate's voice boomed through the hallway. My little parlor trick might have stopped him momentarily, but he'd be back. In the meantime, his henchmen would be clamoring to get to me. I'd be a big score for them to get their hands on.

I turned toward the bathroom and blocking the door was one of Nate's hell pups. Only I never would have cuddled with this snarling beast. The poodle's two heads reached the height of my shoulder, and if it stood on its hind legs, it would've dwarfed me, not that that was a major accomplishment seeing as I was only 5"2.

Both heads bared their long, canine fangs that dripped with pink saliva. Red foam caked the corners of each head's mouth. The poodle's black and red curly fur looked like a perm gone bad. I couldn't tell if the red patches were blood, but I refused to get close enough to see.

I pulled out my Walther PPK, aimed and fired once into each head. The hell dog squealed both times, then dropped across the threshold of the bathroom. I approached cautiously, ensuring it was dead before I stepped over it and went inside.

Moving close to the mirror, I removed the black satchel from my neck and poured the bag's contents into my hand. The two crystals rolled between my fingers. The white now held a hint of pink because Hell tainted its purity. This was one of the reasons I'd had to hurry to get out. I knew the longer the crystals stayed in this realm, the quicker they would become useless, and I needed them to get home.

I smashed the crystals against the mirror, hoping they still worked. The crystals shattered, but instead of crumbling to dust, the particles attached to the mirror, making a portal that I quickly climbed through. Just as I fell into the bathroom of the Lusty Crow, the portal shut.

I landed on my knees, letting go of the kitten just before slamming my palms flat on the floor. The trussed up little ball of fur rolled into a pair of men's tennis shoes.

A man's hand reached down and scooped up the kitten, and I realized I had ended up in the men's bathroom instead of the women's. I glanced up, dreading having to explain to the man what had just happened. Fortunately, the man was Jack, but instead of being pleased to see me, he looked pissed.

***

The Lusty Crow
Watson, LA
Friday, December 22nd, 10:00 PM
Countdown: 9 Days 17 Hours 59 Minutes 59 Seconds

Jack reached down and grabbed my arm, helping me up off the floor. "Do you realize you've been gone for twelve hours?" Anger laced his words.

"Really? Felt like twelve minutes to me." I washed my hands, making sure to lather extensively. Touching the bathroom floor had grossed me out as much as that spider had.

"Is that supposed to be a joke?" he asked.

"No. One minute in Hell is equivalent to one hour here on Earth." I turned off the water, pulled towels from the dispenser and dried my hands. Tossing the paper in the garbage, I pulled the key out of my pocket and dangled it in front of him. "I got this back, so whatever time I lost was worth it."

Jack handed me the kitten, took the key, and turned it over to read the inscription on the back. "How are we going to find out what the owl and I3413 mean?"

Shrugging, I took the bindings off the poor kitten and tucked her into the crook of my left arm. He handed the key back to me, and I put it back in my pocket.

"Let's go run it through the Internet."

He followed me out of the bathroom, through the crowded bar and to my office. I booted up the laptop, logged onto the Net and typed the inscription into my favorite search engine. Jack moved a chair beside me and watched as I clicked through pages and pages of physical addresses and genealogy websites before I gave up and ran a search on *owl*. More pages of mundane information popped up. After surfing through more crap, I sat back and petted the kitten while she slept on my lap.

Jack keyed in *owl* and the entire riddle. Tons of information on etiquette tips for ladies and gentlemen popped up. I typed in *owl* and *vampire*. At the bottom of the page, I clicked on a link that led to information on the screech owl and vampires, but it didn't spark anything. So I typed in *screech owl and vampires*, but before I could hit enter, the door flew open.

Ben rushed in and shut the door behind him. "Glad to see you finally made it back, but Miss Mouse is about to leave."

"She's here? Well, that would've been nice to know," I mumbled. "Can you stall her?"

Ben smiled like a school boy with a secret. "Already did. I *accidentally* spilled a drink on her. She is cleaning up in the bathroom."

I pushed away from the desk. "This research is going nowhere anyway. Jack, do you want to go with me while I tail this chick?"

Before he could answer, his cell vibrated with an incoming text. He checked it and gave me a sad smile. "Can't. Gotta take care of something with Dusty."

My shoulders slumped a little, but I quickly recovered and hoped Ben didn't notice. The idea of going on a stake out with him had been very appealing, but if he had something else to do …

"See you tomorrow then," I said.

"Yep," Jack grinned. He pulled his truck keys out of his pocket and swung them around his finger. "The delivery truck's supposed to be here at 10 am, right?"

"Yep," I replied.

"I'll be here. Later."

He left out of the back door, and I followed Ben into the bar just as Miss Mouse and her chosen mate for the night slipped out the front door. I handed the kitten to Ben. "Take care of her for me."

"Sure thing. What's her name?" he asked.

As I hadn't given it any thought until now, I went with the first thing that popped into my head. "Midnight."

"I will guard her with my life," Ben smiled. He bent his head over the kitten, rubbing her forehead with his finger. "Come on. I know where there's some cold milk."

Knowing I left the young animal in good hands, I dashed back to the office for my helmet, cell phone and keys. After the backdoor closed behind me, I locked it and eased over to the edge of the building. Taking a deep breath, I peeked around the corner. Miss Mouse and her date got into a red Dodge Caravan.

Was this some soccer mom turned bad? Maybe ... or maybe I was wrong, and Miss Mouse was just a soccer mom leading a double life. Even though the bracelet wasn't sending any angel-signals, but I hoped she was the woman scorned. I wanted to solve the riddle.

The van headed north and away from any possibility of going to one of the hotels by Interstate 12. This was a good sign for me. If Miss Mouse had gone to a hotel, I'd have suspected she was just into one night stands. *So yay for me.*

Twenty minutes later, she turned right onto a dirt road. I flipped off my lights and pulled onto the shoulder. The mailbox was a dead giveaway the road was a driveway, which curved into a thick forest. The van's taillights blinked out of sight, and I followed.

Trees lined both sides, and I felt like Dorothy in the Land of Oz. I wished my faithful pup was with me, but I knew Kate would take a bite out of me if I ever called her Toto.

After I rounded the second curve, I turned off the bike and pushed it the rest of the way. The third curve was the last, and the driveway led to an open field. The house sat in the middle of a vast amount of cleared land, and the forest surrounded all sides. I was glad that I had cut off the motor. It would've been hard explaining what I was doing there.

The van stopped by the Victorian farm house. The motor cut off, and both occupants got out. Miss Mouse led the way onto the porch. Her keys rattled as she opened the door, and after her *date* slipped inside the darkened structure, she looked back in my direction.

I felt certain she couldn't see me because of the trees, but I froze until she moved into the house. Breathing a sigh of relief, I parked my bike as far off the driveway as possible. I didn't want someone coming down the driveway and unexpectedly running it over, although, my gut instinct told me no one else was coming. I sat next to a tree.

I could have broken into the house, but I had no good cause to. The man entered of his own free will. My plan was to see if he exited it of his own free will as well.

I tried to tune my hearing to the sounds inside the house, but I was unsuccessful. It wasn't that it was too far away, but something blocked it. I wondered what kind of spell it was and spent the next hour trying to get past it and going over spells I knew. None seemed to match, and I began to wonder if maybe it was someone's power instead of a spell.

The hours dragged, and I wondered what Dusty needed Jack's help with. If the text was even from Dusty … it could've been from one of the twins. Heck, it could've been from both of the twins for all I knew.

Jealousy reared its ugly head, and I battled it away. Jack was not mine. He wore big boy pants and didn't need a nanny. Not that I intended to be one. *A naughty nanny maybe …*

I blew a strand of hair out of my eyes. *Seriously, Angelle. Get a grip. You can't have a relationship these days that doesn't involve sex. And you can't have that if you want to get into Heaven. So get over him.*

But that is, of course, easier said than done.

The second the sun rose, Miss Mouse and her guest exited the house. My bike and I were well hidden in the bushes, and after the van drove past, I took my time leaving the premises. I wanted to make sure they were gone and didn't see me.

The night wasn't a waste. I was happy the guy had walked away of his own accord, which meant that perhaps Miss Mouse wasn't draining men of their blood. Unfortunately, the metaphoric arrow of suspicion pointing to Miss Mouse spun wildly in the opposite direction. Perhaps she wasn't the woman scorned, but I was still determined to keep a close eye on her.

***

CHAPTER 12

The Lusty Crow
Watson, LA
Saturday, December 23rd, 10:00 PM
Countdown: 8 Days 17 Hours 59 Minutes 59 Seconds

Pete sat at the bar with a drink in his hand. Miss Mouse sat beside him, and they chatted. Fifteen minutes passed, and they got up and left. I grabbed my keys and vampire slaying bag, went out the back door and got in the passenger side of Kate's Mustang. She revved the engine.

In no time at all, we were at the driveway of Miss Mouse's house. Kate parked on the side of the road, and we walked down the driveway to the clearing and sat side by side while waiting for Pete's signal. The trees camouflaged us.

It was a long, long wait. In fact, when the sun hit the sky, I started worrying. He didn't come out of the house.

"Demon-wings," I muttered. Something was wrong.

"Where is he? Do you see him?" Kate jumped to her feet and peered between the trees.

"D-wings, d-wings, d-wings." I stood, and my fingernails dug into my palms. "He should've come out by now."

"Angelle." Kate's voice shook, and her green eyes swirled with worry. "What does that mean?"

"It means our plan just took a few left turns."

Reaching into the bag, I pulled out two garlic necklaces and vampire stakes. I handed Kate the wooden stake and kept the silver one for myself. I held it out jokingly. "Unless you want this one?"

"Yeah, allergic to silver, remember?"

I smiled despite the grim situation. "Just kidding."

We stepped onto the front porch and hesitated in front of the door. We both took a deep breath, and I glanced at her.

"Well, let's save Pete's ass."

Thankfully, the front door was unlocked. I hated breaking and entering.

The dark foyer loomed before us, and the house was quieter than Miss Mouse herself. The smell of fresh and dying flowers filled my nose, but there was a different odor of decay beneath the flowery scent.

The stairs were on my left, and I was once again grateful I didn't need a flashlight. All the windows had been painted black, and the inside of the house reminded me of a mausoleum. At the end of the first flight of stairs, I had the choice of going back down on my right or continuing up on my left. I kept climbing with Kate right behind me.

My hand trailed against the smooth wooden banister. The hair on the back of my neck rose, and goose bumps riddled my arms.

I paused at the top of the stairs and stared into a vacant bedroom. I cocked my head and listened to the drip-drip-drip of a leaking faucet. I tried to pick up on the sound of people breathing or of heartbeats but could only hear Kate. Where the hell was Pete?

After we searched all four bedrooms along with their respective closets and private bathrooms, Kate and I searched the first floor and ended in the kitchen.

"Why are there so many decaying flowers?" Kate whispered.

118

I glanced around the kitchen. Molding foliage sprouted from every nook and cranny, and it reminded me of an abandoned funeral parlor. "No clue. Let's check out the garage."

Opening the door, I winced as it creaked loud enough to wake the dead roses. A set of stairs on my left led up to a bonus room over the garage.

"Sweet," I whispered, setting each foot carefully on the carpeted steps. At the top, the locked door did nothing to deter me. Since we were already in the house, I considered my next action to be more of a rescue mission instead of breaking and entering as I could now hear Pete's low breathing.

I twisted the knob until it broke off in my hand and pushed the door open wide. It creaked as well, but I was past caring.

The room glowed in soft candle light, and a closed, mahogany coffin took up most of the area. Pete was chained to the wall on the other side, and the pure silver cuffs singed his flesh, sending out tendrils of smoke above his wrists. His chin touched his chest, and I caught a whiff of wolfsbane hanging around his neck. Clearly, his Werewolf scent had given him away.

Kate rushed past me and ripped the chains from the wall, hissing from making contact with silver. She lowered Pete to the floor, took off the necklace of wolfsbane and tossed it across the room. Right away, he started to come around.

"Wha – where am I?" He looked around in confusion.

"Do you remember anything?" she asked.

"No."

Breaking the silver cuffs from his burnt wrists, I dropped them on the ground, stood and turned to the coffin. "Get him out of here, Kate. Take him home and fix him up. I'll be right behind you."

My voice sounded otherworldly even to me. Kate didn't ask any questions and half-carried, half-guided Pete out of the room.

Obviously, Miss Mouse knew the blood of a Werewolf could help a vampire walk in the daylight. Why else would she have kept him when she'd let all the other men go? The more pertinent question was why did she care? I had seen her in the sun and knew she wasn't a full vampire yet.

Standing over the coffin, I noted that the room was set up like a movie set. The first thing a sire usually teaches its fledgling is not to believe all the movie hype, so I began to think Miss Mouse did not have one. Maybe they had started to turn her but something happened. This had me completely baffled. Crosses don't work, and vampires can see themselves in the mirror. They don't turn into bats, and they cannot read minds. Garlic, however, did work, and stakes did a wonderful job of scattering their dusted bodies all over the floor.

I took the garlic necklace from around my neck, pushed up the coffin lid, and tossed it onto the vampire inside. It would keep her weak against my attack. I raised the stake high but hesitated when I looked at the vampire's face. It wasn't Miss Mouse, but a horribly disfigured version of her dressed in a white satin wedding gown. The vampire had to be Miss Mouse's sister.

Miss Mouse must be a slave to her sister. It was the only explanation that made sense for Miss Mouse to smell like a human and a vampire at the same time.

The young vampire glared at me with hate in her eyes, and I was glad the garlic stopped her from rising and attacking me.

Scars crisscrossed the right side of her face. After a second of staring, it became clear her disfigurement was exactly like the one on the TV in my office. Red spider webs zigzagged from her chin to her forehead. It reminded me of a cracked vase I had at home.

I raised the stake higher. "May God have mercy on your soul."

"Don't kill me. I'm not evil," the vampire bride whispered through parched lips.

I faltered at her words. Was she right? She hadn't actually killed anyone that I knew of, and then it dawned on me she had. Hence the smell of decaying flesh which wasn't hers, and the need for flowers to cover the scent.

My lips pursed, and my eyes narrowed. "Liar. I smell the dead bodies within your walls."

I slammed the stake into her chest and held my breath as dust exploded like a water bomb. I shook my head free of the vampire's ashes before allowing myself a satisfied grin. Clearly Miss Mouse was the lady in waiting who brought gentlemen to the scorned bride, her very own sister.

"Okay, Robert. It's done. The riddle is solved and staked."

I heard movement behind me and turned around, expecting to see Robert's shimmering form. I was ecstatic I had solved his riddle and saved my soul.

However, the only thing shimmering was the back of a shovel as it slammed into my face. The force of it would have killed a normal human. For me, it simply knocked me unconscious.

***

Miss Mouse's House
Watson, LA
Sunday, December 24th, 4:00 PM
Countdown: 7 Days 23 Hours 59 Minutes 59 Seconds

I woke to a throbbing nose. My chin was sticky with my blood. Several teeth felt lose, and I swore I'd knock some out of whomever had hit me. Payback is a demon named Bitch, after all.

My swollen eyes only opened a mere slit. I was still in the bonus room, and I was shackled to the wall as Pete had been earlier. My arms were stretched above my head. I tested the cuffs, but they remained magically reinforced.

"When your neck didn't break from the force of the shovel hitting your face, I took necessary precautions," said a woman.

The voice floated from somewhere in front of me. I could barely make out a figure a few yards away. The strain of trying to see hurt, so I closed my eyes and let my chin hang over my chest. I had an awful headache, and it didn't improve when she slapped me.

"Hey," I snarled between split lips.

The tip of something pressed against my chest. When I looked, I saw it was the silver stake I had used to dust the vampire bride.

"Ever wonder what it feels like?" Miss Mouse hissed.

"No, not particularly."

"Well, when I get through with you, you'll be begging to be staked." The point dug painfully into me.

"Make mine medium rare." My tongue felt swollen.

"What?" she snapped.

"My steak … medium rare."

"Cute … but you won't be for long."

She stepped close, and I could smell the rot in her soul. She pressed the sharp tip of the stake to my cheek. I jumped from the icy coldness. "Did you see the lovely scars on my sister's face?"

"Hard to miss."

She sliced open my cheek, and I winced, refusing to give her the satisfaction of a scream. Warm blood trickled down. "So why do you smell like both vampire and human?"

She hesitated. "Probably because my sister never bit me. I just drank her blood. It gives me power."

"So in essence, you were her bitch," I mumbled.

The tip of the stake sliced my chin, and I gritted my teeth, forcing down the pain.

Make a note, Angelle. Never antagonize your captor. They tend to Stake it out on you.

Grabbing my hair, she slammed my head against the wall. "I served my sister well. She promised to make me a vampire, but you screwed that up for me."

Miss Mouse *was* pretty much screwed. Once a human drank from a vampire, they became blood addicts, which were pretty much like drug addicts, except for the part where they die if they don't get their fix. There's no kicking the need for vampire blood, and I prayed Jack wasn't an addict.

"What happened to your sister's sire?" I asked.

She snorted and dug another line into my face. She was getting busy drawing patterns on my cheek, and yes, it hurt like Hell. However, I wasn't giving her any satisfaction by voicing my pain.

"Her bitch of a sire stole my sister's husband and her soul."

I wanted to say *false*. Vampires don't lose their soul when turned. It only makes the evil in a person more pronounced and hard to fight. I clenched my teeth as she dug into my flesh. I wasn't worried. It would heal.

"I'm guessing her sire scarred up her face."

"Oh, yes. My sister Audrey was left for dead, but her rotten stinking groom turned her. I took care of him, though, and his skanky mistress aka Audrey's sire. Those are two vampires who'll never see the dark of night again."

So she dusted them. Fitting.

123

"So would you say she was a woman scorned?" I tried to distract myself from her vigilant carving on my face.

"Yep."

Okay, Robert, where are you? I've solved the riddle, now save my sorry ass.

I knew better. He couldn't interfere or even appear until I was alone. I was on my own, positive Kate had forgotten about me in her effort to get Pete back to normal. "So how many dead bodies you got crammed in the walls?"

She hesitated. "You sure are nosy."

"I've been told that before." I blinked back the cloudy vision, grateful I could finally see.

Miss Mouse froze with her top lip curled up. "You're not squirming … and you haven't made a sound. I know this has to hurt."

I shrugged. "What can I say? I've got a high threshold for pain."

My neck was sticky, and my clothes were ruined. I pulled on the chains with everything I had. "Where'd you get these things?"

"From a witch. Aren't they cool? There's a spell on them to help keep evil locked up."

My smirk faded. I was still evil? No way.

My hope faltered. But what about all the good I've done? The souls I've saved? It occurred to me that the baddies don't ever see themselves as evil.

The words of my pastor floated in my head. *'Man shall not be saved by good works alone … but by faith in Jesus Christ.'*

"Aw, what's wrong?" Miss Mouse cooed. "Didn't think you were evil, did you? Just because you dust vampires doesn't make you good, lady."

"Yeah, you would know. Let me lock you in these and see how you like it."

"I'm not evil, so they wouldn't work."

I raised my left eyebrow. Talk about deluded. "Stuffing dead bodies in the wall sure constitutes an act of evil."

Her eyes narrowed. "Those men were evil. They deserved to die."

"Maybe … but not by your hand."

Her lips curled up into a sneer. "Who are you? God?"

My lips clamped together. I wasn't about to tell her of my previous fallen angel status. She'd probably try to do something stupid like drink my blood. I'd rather she kill me.

She silently assessed my lack of response. "You're not a vampire. Not a demon." She sniffed my hair. "Smells like … human. You must be a witch."

I gave her my best evil smile. "Good guess. Kill me, and my coven will cast a spell on you that'll make you wish you weren't going to live forever."

"What the hell?" She tilted her head and dug the blade's tip into my healing skin. "So you've a healing spell on you. Nice one. But let's see if you heal from this."

Before I could utter a word, she took the stake … *my* stake … and shoved it deep into my chest. I screamed. My hands clenched as the need to pull it out raced through me. My hands were still cuffed, so that wasn't happening.

I looked down at the blood gushing everywhere. I still heard myself screaming, but it was as if I were listening to a movie. The room seemed to shrink and fade. I was suddenly at the end of a tunnel, and I couldn't believe that the bitch had staked me. The last thing I heard was - "Your coven can kiss my ass."

***

Scorned

CHAPTER 13

Angelle's Bedroom
Watson, LA
Wednesday, December 27th, 4:00 PM
Countdown: 4 Days 23 Hours 59 Minutes 59 Seconds

Someone rocked me. Warm arms held me tight. Nausea rolled over me, and I squeezed my eyes shut.

Stop.

The word didn't make it past my lips. I tried again.

"Stop."

I knew it sounded weak, but it worked. My world quit moving, and I sank back into the dark, only to be yanked up by the sound of Jack's voice. It rumbled through his chest and into my body.

"Angelle … please wake up."

His voice was music to my soul, but I couldn't figure out why it sounded funny. There was a sense of pleading in those four little words, and it piqued my curiosity. Why did such a strong man sound like he was crying? It was horribly heart wrenching. I found the strength to peek at him.

Jack's face was inches from mine. I was on his lap and wrapped up in his arms. His baby blues locked with mine, and I watched the fear in them brighten to hope. He smiled as joy lit his previously heartbroken face.

I reached up to swipe at a tear trailing down his cheek. He'd been crying, and I didn't know why. Something had happened, and I searched my memory but came up blank. The fuzzies started swarming in my vision, and I closed my eyes to shake them off. My hand fell on my chest, and the sweet warmth of dark oblivion pulled at me.

"She's going to be fine," I heard Jack say before all conscious thought faded away. It seemed like only minutes had passed before I woke again.

I cracked open an eye, pleased to see Jack's sleeping face next to mine. His sensuous mouth was relaxed, and no lines marred his features. He looked like he hadn't a care in the world.

Cross tattoo. I immediately looked at my right breast, confirming that it was still there. If Miss Mouse had jammed the stake through the cross, I would be waking up next to Nate instead of Jack. Beneath the tattoo was a tiny vial of poison that even my super healing couldn't cure.

Jack still slept. Apparently, he had taken care of me while I healed. Did this mean his opinion of non-human beings was changing? The memory of him and Dusty trying to sun-dust me popped into my head. He could have let me die. He could have finished the job Miss Mouse had started, but he didn't.

My heart softened. Was this what love felt like? It had been so long since I had felt anything but lust. I had fought the losing battle with my libido for so long that I wasn't sure what love was.

Jack's eyes popped open, and I smiled.

"Hey."

He returned my grin. "Hi."

We laid there and stared at each other. I licked my dry lips. "So I get pillow talk without having done the deed. That's a switch."

Lust darkened his eyes. "Believe me, your luscious curves were hard to resist waking you up. What do you remember?"

I grimaced. "Everything. Where's Miss Mouse?"

"Arrested and in jail for multiple counts of murder."

"She won't live that long. She's hooked on vamp blood, and without it …" I drew a line across my throat.

He froze for the briefest of seconds. Something strange flitted through his eyes, but he eased off the bed before I could see more. A sudden fear pierced my heart as things clicked into place.

"Please tell me you didn't drink the twins' blood."

My voice cracked with terror. I watched him closely as he put on his shoes. He'd slept with his clothes on, and while I was touched over his concern for me, the sweetness of it became lost to the fear that he was now a human slave. Pain constricted my heart and twisted it violently as I waited for his answer.

He scoffed at me. "That's absurd. Why would I do something stupid like that?"

I didn't believe him even though I deeply wanted to. Pushing aside the desire to weep, I slapped on a happy face. Blood addicts would lie to their mother, so there was no use thinking he wouldn't lie to me.

He moved to sit beside me. "How's your chest feel?"

"Fine … I'm just tired. How long was I out?"

"Three days. You missed Christmas." He picked up a wrapped box on the nightstand and put it in my hands. "It's just something that caught my eye when I went to the grocery store the other day."

"I didn't get you anything," I mumbled as I tore off the wrapping paper.

Jack shrugged. "It's not about the getting."

The paper fell on my lap, and I held up the glass blown Magnolia. There was no way in the world he could have known this was my favorite flower.

"This is beautiful," I said. "Thank you."

"You're welcome."

The black kitten chose that moment to jump onto the bed and planted her butt in my lap. She looked bigger than when I had last seen her. At that time, she had been the size of a can of soda. Now, her size equaled that of a toaster. Three days shouldn't have made that much of a difference. Her green eyes looked into mine, and she began purring. Was there more to this cat than what met the eye? She had come from another realm, so anything was possible.

"I guess we've solved the riddle," I said.

"How so?" Jack asked as he petted the kitten.

"Miss Mouse was bringing men home for her sister to feed on. Apparently, the sister is the woman scorned because her newly-wedded husband had a vampire mistress."

"So if you solved the riddle, why are you still wearing that?" Jack pointed at the bracelet on my arm.

My heart skipped a beat as I stopped scratching Midnight's ears and touched the gold bracelet. Jack was right. It should have disappeared.

"You're right. I've gotta talk to Robert." I peeked under the covers to ensure I was clothed. Thankfully, I had on a long LSU t-shirt and flannel pajama bottoms.

"Kate cleaned you up," Jack stated.

"Good to know."

Moving the kitten to the floor, I stood, and Jack rushed to where I stood. He pulled me into his arms and crushed me to him. I was surprised at first but wrapped my arms around him and held on. He didn't say anything for a moment, and I let his unspoken feelings for me soak into my soul.

It was hard to remember we'd only known each other for a short time. I have an excellent memory, but I didn't remember certain things from my life as an angel. His soul was old, but I had never met him in one of his past lives.

"I can't shake the sight of that stake sticking out of your chest," Jack whispered into my hair. "All that blood. I thought you were dead."

"Well, I was worried there for a while myself before I passed out." I remained locked in his arms, and my bladder started to protest. "This feels great, but before I call Robert, I have to go to the bathroom."

He immediately let go and stepped back. "Sorry."

I shuffled toward the bathroom, glad he took my elbow to keep me from falling. He let go of me at the doorway and asked, "Are you hungry? I can rustle you up some eggs while you talk to Robert."

My stomach rumbled. "Oooo, sounds yummy. Scrambled?"

"Whatever you want."

"Thanks." I shut the door and took care of business.

Before I called Robert, I inspected the white, homemade bandage in the center of my chest. There was a large spot of red in the middle of it ... my blood. I picked at the tape holding it in place and grimaced as it pulled skin. I held my breath and ripped it away.

My flesh was smooth as a baby's. I ran my fingers over where the hole should have been and wondered what it had looked like. There wasn't even a scar.

I sighed and adjusted my shirt back into place. Turning off the lights, I said, "Robert."

Almost instantly, the demon appeared by the door. He held a half-eaten hamburger in his right hand and a drink in the other. A dab of ketchup graced his chin. I tossed him a towel and said, "You could've cleaned up first."

He simply shrugged. "Are you okay? I heard you got staked."

"I'm fine. Just glad I solved the riddle."

"I'm sorry to be the bearer of bad news, but you haven't solved the riddle."

My heart sank, and I let out a heavy sigh. "I was afraid of that."

"Sorry." Robert's form started to shimmer. "I have to go. I was actually on a date when you called me."

Demon smoke filled my nose as the lights flipped back on. Depressed, I opened the bathroom door and almost stepped on the kitten. Scooping Midnight into my arms, I smelled burning eggs and walked into the kitchen,

Burnt smoke rose from the eggs that still cooked on the stove, and I quickly turned it off before my house went up in flames.

"Seriously, Jack?" I asked, as I turned to look at him.

He stood unmoving in the middle of the room. His right hand was raised, and he had a death grip on the spatula.

What the demon-wings?

***

Angelle's Kitchen
Watson, LA
Wednesday, December 27th, 6:00 PM
Countdown: 4 Days 21 Hours 59 Minutes 59 Seconds

"Jack?"

I stepped close and waved my hand in front of his glassed-over eyes. He didn't respond. *What's going on here?*

A loud crash reverberated throughout the house, and I jumped. Midnight scratched me in her mad leap from my arms, and she ran off to find a hiding place. Leaving Jack in the kitchen, I ran into the living room.

Broken glass littered the floor, and a patio chair lay in the middle of the room with its legs up in the air. The large window that overlooked the back porch was destroyed, and the cold, night air blasted in.

My blood boiled. *Broken halos. I just had that window replaced about a month ago. There's gonna be some Hell-paying.*

I shivered once from the cold and once more from anger. In the darkness, bodies moved out of my vision before I could discern who they were.

"What the demon-wings do you think you're doing?" I yelled. "Who are you, and what do you want?"

"Why don't you come outside and find out?" taunted a feminine voice.

I recognized it as one of the twins, and I narrowed my eyes. "Um, yeah. I'll take a rain check."

"Oh, Jack, come out and play with us," sang Marishka.

He ran past me and out the back door before I could stop him. Marishka forced him to sit in a chair that she had placed in front of the broken window. His actions reaffirmed my fear that he was a blood addict, and my heart sank.

Marishka draped herself around him from behind, and she bared her fangs inches above his neck. Her sister stepped in front of them, blocking my view. Trina smirked at me. "Want your friend back? Then come and get him."

I knew better then to walk into a trap, but what else could I do? I stepped toward the back door and into a spot I knew she couldn't see me. I reached behind a picture on the wall and pulled out a small silver knife. It wasn't much defense, but it was all I had time to grab.

Remaining in the area between the window and the door, I grabbed the doorknob, twisted and pulled it open. Something liquid sprayed over the threshold and into the area that I would have been standing had I opened the door the normal way. *Thank God for smart thinking.*

I grabbed the arm holding the pink pepper spray can and tried to pull Trina in. However, the minute her hand entered my home without a verbal invite, her well-manicured fingers curled up into an old hag's hand. The skin wrinkled and turned grey.

Since Trina hadn't asked permission to enter my home, her body was becoming zombified. This meant her body would be slow and dull-witted and easy to kill.

Trina yanked her arm back quicker than I could let go, and I was pulled through the door and fell on my knees. *What the demon-wings? Why is she stronger than me?*

Trina held the rotten hand in front of her face. "What did you do to my hand?" she screamed. Terror twisted her pretty features, revealing a bit of the vampire beneath her skin. Her fangs dropped, and she hissed.

Before I could answer, she grabbed me by the neck with her good hand and pulled me up until my feet dangled in the air. My breath cut off, and I slashed at her arm with the knife. The blade sliced into her, and its silver singed her flesh.

Marishka appeared beside us and grabbed my hand that held the knife. She pried my fingers away from the blade and tossed it out into the yard.

With a wicked smile, Marishka held up a syringe. "Nighty night time."

She stretched out my arm and jabbed the needle into a vein. She pushed down on the syringe's plunger, and the fluid crashed into my body.

Ice flooded through me. The paralyzing cold swept down my arms and spread throughout my body until I could no longer move. Terror spun over me as the drug took control of my body. My body relaxed, and I stopped fighting.

"I heard you liked elephant tranquilizers," one of the vampires whispered in my ear.

Jack, why would you tell them this?

As my legs turned to dead weight, I was doubly glad I hadn't revealed the secret of my tattoo. If the tiny vial beneath it were broken, the poison in it would kill me.

Trina shook me. "Jack is ours, and you are toast."

With her hand still around my throat, she carried me down the steps and dropped me by the small pond. She and Marishka bound my legs and hands and tied an anchor around my waist. They picked me up and swung me between them like a hammock blowing in the wind. When they let go of me, I flew weightless through the air.

I landed in the middle of the pond, and the icy water bit through to my bones. The anchor pulled me to the bottom. I panicked, but without the ability to move, there was nothing to do but suck nasty water into my mouth and nose. My lungs filled with water and burned with the need for air. Darkness wavered at the edge of my consciousness, and I struggled to remain awake. Unfortunately, the drug still had me immobile. I couldn't do anything until it wore off.

Jack.

The fact that he lied to me hurt more than the water in my lungs.

Why are you surprised? You should be used to having a man hurt you. Remember how Nate betrayed you? He used your own naivety against you. Took your love, turned it to lust and made you believe it was true love.

A tear slid out of my eye and drifted away in the water. *Maybe Jack isn't like that.*

He tried to fry you in the sun when he thought you were a vampire. The darker side of my nature argued with me.

Actually, that had been Dusty. Jack had suggested staking, a quicker death. I reasoned with myself.

And that's better? my darker self asked sarcastically.

Well, he did offer to take me to the ER when I sliced my finger open, and he did help me check out Kate when the car hit us. I reminded myself.

And he told the twins what drug to use against you. Now you're lying at the bottom of a pond while they ride off into the moonlight. He's not that much different than Nate – in my opinion.

Damn my darker self.

In the beginning, Nate's sweet and boyish charm had lured me in hook, line and sinker. After we had fallen, Nate made love to me for the first time. Neither of us had found it satisfying. He disappeared from Hell for a few days, and when he came back, he brought a harlot from a brothel. He made me learn everything she knew and then some. After I became an expert in sex, he couldn't get enough of my tricks … said he loved me and gave me the Lust demons to oversee.

I lived that way for so long that I became blinded by lust. Nate taught me how to use a human's desires and even fears to get them to turn away from Love and follow Lust straight into Hell.

But one day I tempted the wrong man. He had simply smiled and said that while I was lovely, his wife rivaled the sun's sparkle on crystal water. His heart and his passion belonged to his wife, who in truth was not very beautiful but had a kind heart and pure soul. The minute I looked upon the woman, I understood.

The man had gazed upon his homely wife with love.

I looked into his heart, and I saw that true love saw beauty where there was none in the flesh. There had been no room in his heart for lust because true love had encompassed all of it.

I left then – went back to Hell. The idea of true love plagued me, and I looked at Nate with new eyes. He fell short in every aspect. Every "kindness" from Nate became manipulative. He had never loved me for he loved himself more.

No man deserves my heart. I felt as scorned as the bride I hunted.

The memory of Jack's smile flashed in my mind. His twinkling blue eyes warmed my heart, and the memory of the way he laughed made me smile. I had only known him for a short time, but sometimes it only takes a moment to connect with someone.

What were those vamps planning on doing with him? He needed saving, and while I could lie at the bottom of this pond for eternity, he was mortal.

The ability to move had returned. I easily broke the ropes around my wrists as well as the ones tying me to the anchor and around my legs. Planting my bare feet in the pond's mushy muddy bottom, I slowly rose out of the water. Fortunately for me, the pond was only four feet deep. So the joke was on the stupid vamps who thought they'd drown me in my own backyard.

The vamps and Jack were gone. I trudged out of the pond, shivering as the wind cut through my wet clothing. The grass tickled the bottom of my feet as I went over to the water hose and sprayed the mud off. Looking around the side of the house, I saw that Jack's truck was gone.

Fear gnawed at my guts, and I ran onto the back porch and into the house. Quickly changing into dry clothes, I took the owl key out of my wet jeans pocket, put it on a sturdy necklace and hung it around my neck. As I went back in to the living room, I tucked the key under my t-shirt. Picking up the overturned patio chair, I surveyed the broken window, wondering what to do about that. For the moment, nothing. I had to go after Jack and the twins while the trail was fresh.

Grabbing my weapons, cell phone and bike keys, I dashed out the front door and down the steps. I stopped dead in my tracks at the sight before me. My bike lay in two pieces.

Those bitches had broken her in half.

***

CHAPTER 14

Angelle's House
Watson, LA
Wednesday, December 27th, 10:00 PM
Countdown: 4 Days 17 Hours 59 Minutes 59 Seconds

I sat on the steps of the porch, waiting for Kate, my weredog best friend. Since my only mode of transportation had been trashed, I needed a ride to Jack's motel room. While I waited for Kate, I had tried calling Dusty, but it went straight to voicemail.

Kate's black Mustang pulled in to the driveway and stopped in front of me. The headlights blinded me as I dashed to the passenger door and climbed in. "Let's go."

"Where?"

"To Jack's hotel room. Maybe Dusty's there. I tried calling him, but he didn't answer. If he's not there, I'm gonna pick the lock and have a peek. I wish I knew where the twins lived, or rather, unlived."

It didn't take long to get to the cheap motel in Denham Springs. Traffic wasn't as bad as it was during rush hour, but there were still plenty of vehicles roaming Florida Boulevard.

Kate pulled into the parking lot of The Cottage Inn Motel, taking the first entrance between the motel's office building and a two story building of rooms on the right.

We were interested in the single story building on the left. I knew of the seedy motel. I felt sorry for the few real tourists who got suckered into staying there. It was a well-known prostitute and drug haven, and I hated the fact Jack stayed at the place.

I banged on the door, hoping nobody would answer. I was looking for an excuse to be able to break in and search for clues. That wasn't meant to be.

"Take your tricks someplace else, honey," grunted a tired voice from the other side of the door. "I told you earlier I wasn't interested."

"Dusty, it's Angelle. I'm looking for Jack."

There was a millisecond of silence. "He's supposed to be nursing you back to health."

"He did, but the twin vampires kidnapped him. Can I come in? I'd rather not discuss this with a door between us."

Kate tapped my elbow, and I looked to my right. A shadowy figure walked toward us. My skin pricked with unease. I really didn't want to have to fight right now. I still felt drained.

The locks on the other side of the door snapped, and I pushed Kate inside just as the approaching person called out.

"We're not interested," I stated.

The person cursed under their breath but turned away. Nonetheless, I rushed into the room and slammed the door shut, quickly taking care of locking it up as well.

Turning to Dusty, I smiled. "You should've been named Nick."

"Huh?"

"As in the Nick of time ..." My dry sense of humor was lost on the guy. I waved my hand in the air. "Never mind."

Dusty held a pillow in front of his otherwise naked, lanky frame. He wore only a cowboy hat. I raised my left eyebrow. "No, don't get dressed on our account."

He backed into the bathroom. "I'll be right back."

The room had two beds. The bedspread on one was untouched, and the one closest to the bathroom was wrinkled. Take out boxes and other trash littered the room. I noticed a suitcase peeking out from under Dusty's bed, and I wondered if it held clothes or vampire weapons.

Kate touched my arm and motioned to the dresser. A wine glass with lipstick on the rim sat beside a beer bottle. I didn't think there was anyone beside Dusty in the bathroom, but I've been wrong before.

"Hey, Dusty, if you want us to come back later ..." I let my words trail off.

The bathroom door flew open, revealing just Dusty. The shower curtain was pulled back, so nobody hid in the shower. Not that he would care if we knew he had a woman in here.

Now fully dressed in jeans and a t-shirt, he stepped into the area and adjusted his cowboy hat. "Why would you come back later?"

I pointed to the wine glass. "I figured you had company."

He smiled and put on his black duster. "That was last night. I took full advantage of young Jack not being here."

Rolling my eyes, I stepped further away from the beds. "Did Jack mention where the twins live?"

"No, but I installed a tracking devise on his truck without his knowing it. So we can at least find that. Are we taking my truck or yours?"

"Well, I'm not leaving my Mustang here unattended," Kate stated. "I don't want some skank parking her butt on it while she markets her trade."

Starting at his boots, I lifted my gaze up Dusty's tall, six foot four frame. "I seriously doubt you'd want to cram yourself into a little car. How about I ride with you and Kate'll follow us?"

He nodded while grabbing his cell phone, keys, wallet and the tracking device. "Let's go."

Dusty walked out first to make sure the undesirables weren't lurking near our door. There were only a few vehicles in the parking lot. Jack and Dusty's room was the last on the row, and I kept an eye on the couple groping each other on the sidewalk two doors down. I didn't want to be surprised if they tried to attack us. Fortunately, we made it to the vehicles without a single incident.

We took North Range Avenue until it turned into LA Highway 16 and continued north until we were miles past my bar. I wasn't surprised when Dusty took a left onto a dirt road just past the gravel pits.

The truck's headlights cut into the darkness, but even with the high beams on, the light only reached two feet in front of the truck. Tree limbs reached out from the forest, scratching the doors. The tires constantly dipped into large holes, and Dusty took pleasure in hitting each one faster than the last. I held on to the *oh-shit* bar above the passenger door, bracing my foot against the floorboards to help steady myself.

The road was only wide enough for one car, so hopefully none were heading in our direction. Dusty slammed on his brakes, and my body smashed against the seatbelt.

"Seriously?" I snapped. "Maybe slow it down a notch."

"Good idea," he mumbled, making the first of many turns.

Dusty may have thought it a good idea, but he didn't practice it. His constant speeding up and stopping on a dime almost gave me whiplash. I wished I'd ridden with Kate. Fortunately, the headlights finally landed on Jack's truck, and my stomach lurched.

What would we find?

***

Woods
Watson, LA
Thursday, December 28ᵗʰ, 12:00 AM
Countdown: 4 Days 15 Hours 59 Minutes 59 Seconds

Pulling up behind Jack's truck, Dusty killed the engine. I pushed open the passenger door, and the rusty hinges creaked in protest. Sliding to the ground, my boots squished through the mud as I ran to the vehicle.

Dusty beat me there, and he pulled open the driver's door. The cab's light flashed on, beaming down on an empty seat. The egg-covered spatula from my kitchen lay on the floor. He handed it to me, and after shaking off the dried egg, I put it in my back pocket. He stepped away from the truck and pushed the door until it closed with a soft click. Pulling a small flashlight from a pocket in his duster, he used it to survey the area.

Straight ahead lay the river, and the light from the flashlight played over the dark water rushing silently past. Bushes and trees lay to our right. When the light hit a rabbit, it froze until Dusty shown the light elsewhere.

The flashlight illuminated a dilapidated shack on the other side of Jack's truck. I pulled my Walther PPK out of one boot, a small knife from the other and headed for the dwelling with Kate and Dusty behind me. If the place fell on top of us, so be it.

The steps creaked as I went up, stepping over a broken board that used to be the top step. The porch was littered with missing slats, and I imagined all sorts of earthly and otherworldly nasties reaching up to grab our legs.

Dusty shone the flashlight on the broken windows. Spider webs covered most of them, and I shivered.

Hopefully, a giant spider does not live here.

142

Cracked and peeling paint covered the door, which stood partially opened. I pushed it with the toe of my boot, and the door creaked open.

Haunted house, here we come.

A stench hit my nose and stopped me in my tracks. Something had died in the shack and was still there, rotting. I followed the scent to a small room in the back and froze in the doorway.

Blood covered the floor and walls, but upon closer inspection, the blood was dried and old.

"It's not Jack's blood," Kate said. "His scent smells like cinnamon."

Marishka lay on the floor in a pool of blood. A stake protruded from the middle of her chest where her heart was. Why hadn't she exploded into dust?

"She's not dead." Aiming the handgun at her with my right hand, I moved cautiously into the room, balancing the knife in my left hand.

Dusty knelt beside the body, taking vitals, and I tensed, waiting for her to rise. Vampires do have a pulse, but I hoped hers was gone.

"Well, she appears dead," he said. He inspected the stake without removing it. "This is Jack's. His initials are carved in it, which is good. Means he put up a fight."

Kate remained at the door, keeping guard. "I don't trust this. Her body should've exploded into dust on impact."

Something nagged at my memory, which was crap as compared to what it used to be. When I was an angel in all aspects of the word, I remembered everything. Since my humanization, there were only certain things I could recall from that life.

"She didn't explode because she's a born vampire. The only reason she didn't dust is because her *parent* still lives," I said. "I don't recollect how I know this, but this is a different strain of vampire."

143

"So to kill her we have to kill her parent?" Kate asked.

"I think so," I replied. I shook my head in frustration, trying to remember. "The answer is right there on the tip of my wings."

Dusty stood. "Let's test this theory. I have a machete in the truck. We'll start by cutting off her head, and if that doesn't work, we'll try death by sunlight."

"Is it possible they can walk in sunlight?" Kate asked, as Dusty left the room.

I racked my brain. "I don't think so. They'd probably just burn."

He took the light with him, but neither Kate nor I needed light to see in the dark. I listened as his boots echoed down the steps and across the grass. The truck door squealed open. After a few seconds of unnatural silence, my angel-sense tingled.

"Something's wrong," I whispered, refusing to take my eyes off Marishka.

"I'm on it," Kate said.

Just as she left the room, Marishka's left hand twitched. I adjusted my aim, ready for whatever the vampire had to dish out.

"Mother said you'd be hard to kill," Marishka murmured as she pulled the stake from her chest and sat up.

Mother? And one that knows me that well? Shit.

I pulled back the trigger and prepared to fire a round of vampire bullets into Marishka but was interrupted before I could shoot.

"I know you're dead-set on rescuing Jack," said a voice from the doorway.

I jumped, quickly adjusting my position so that I had both vampires in sight. Unfortunately, I was trapped. Raising my chin, I growled, "You bitches broke my bike."

"That's not all we broke," Trina said. She stepped aside, revealing a third female vampire, who held Kate's limp body in her arms. My heart jumped in my throat.

I weighed my options, which weren't many. I could start shooting, but unless the three vampires lined up in a single file, I'd only get a few rounds off before one of them overtook me. Not to mention I'd probably hit Kate.

Directly behind me was a medium sized window, but unlike the other windows in the shack, the glass in this one was completely intact. So jumping out of it would result in a multitude of cuts.

But I'd rather that than suffer a vampire bite.

"What do you want?" I asked, slowly edging toward the window.

"Your cooperation," Trina said and held up a capped syringe. "Our mother wants to talk to you."

"Tell her to text me," I said and threw the knife into Trina's throat.

At the same time, I fired a bullet into Marishka's forehead, whipped around and shot out the window. I dove through it, wincing as the jagged edges of glass scratched my arms.

I landed ungracefully on my shoulder, immediately rolling on my back and aiming the gun at the open window. When nobody appeared to be coming after me, I jumped up, crept around to the front of the shack and peered around a corner.

Dusty lay sprawled on the front porch, guarded by yet another vampire. I debated on going back for them. I was outnumbered, but that had never stopped me before.

Trina and Marishka stepped on to the porch. Neither my knife nor my bullets had kept them down. A foreboding shiver sent goose bumps across my skin, and I retreated into the woods.

The best offense was a good defense. I couldn't save my friends if I was tied up with them, and since these

vampires couldn't be killed by normal means, I turned
tail and ran.

***

CHAPTER 15

Woods
Watson, LA
Thursday, December 28ᵗʰ, 3:00 AM
Countdown: 4 Days 12 Hours 59 Minutes 59 Seconds

Self-preservation fueled my decision to run willy-nilly into the swamp-like woods. Trina and her gang of indestructible vampires required a better plan than "stake em or bake em." I had to get to a safe haven, which did not include my home or the bar. Instinct told me both places were under surveillance.

A musky odor filled the air, indicating a snake was nearby. I slowed my frantic get away pace to a more observant walk. Granted, the cold weather made him slow, but if I stepped on him, he would still sink fangs into me. At the moment, I preferred to avoid the agony of his poison. The closer I got to him, the stronger the musk became. I stopped a couple hundred yards from him and waited for him to slither off.

Running through the woods in winter is much different than in summer. The cold chased away the usual gnats and mosquitoes as well as the muggy heat from the swamp.

Stopping, I pulled my cell phone from my back pocket and secured the spatula in the other pocket, amazed I hadn't lost it. The cell phone had no coverage, so I replaced it in my pocket and continued heading in the direction of the road.

Wind blew through the tops of the trees, and they moaned as they rubbed together. A raccoon scurried away from me as I approached, and a family of possums settled into their underground den next to a cypress tree. A gator hissed and swished his tail as he hustled through the brush. Fortunately, he went towards the Amite River, the opposite direction I was headed.

As I trudged toward what I hoped was the road, I replayed Trina's words over and over. *Our mother wants to talk to you.*

Now who the hell was their mother? And how many *sisters* did they have? Were there any brothers?

I didn't recall leaving any vampires, female or male, left undusted. So how did this one know me, and what did I do to piss her off?

When I stepped out of the swampy woods, I breathed a sigh of relief. The gravel from the shoulder crunched beneath my boots, and my cell phone had bars. I called Ben.

"Those bitches have them all," I growled. "Jack, Dusty, Kate."

"Damn," Ben said. "Where are you?"

"Highway 16 north of the pits." I looked up and down the road to ensure it was empty.

"I'm on my way."

"Ben, I'm worried they're gonna come after you and Pete."

"I can handle myself against some puny vamps," he laughed.

"These are born." I pushed my bangs out of my eyes.

"So am I. At least we know what we are dealing with. Be there in a few."

"Grab my laptop and Pete."

"Okey dokey."

He hung up, and I paced the road, kicking at rocks and feeling useless. I sent a text to my kitchen angel, Vivian.

*Please feed and water Midnight. Vampires might be
back. Protect the house. Please put a magic barrier over
the broken window so nothing gets in until it can be
fixed. Not sure when I will be home.*

Weary, I knelt by the woods, watching the road.
Several cars passed, but none were Ben. He didn't show
up until the sun was close to rising. Pete rode in the
passenger seat of the classic BMW 35CSi 3 Series
Coupe. I climbed into the back of the brown car.

"They broke my bike in half." I crossed my arms and
tried to contain my anger.

"Are you kidding me?" Ben snapped. "Bitches."

Pete twisted around in the passenger seat. His eyes
swirled with wolf. "If they lay one fang on Kate …"

I refrained from saying she was unconscious. Placing
my hand on his shoulder, I said, "We'll get her back."

He simply growled and turned back around. I chewed
my lip, feeling like a heel for not staying to fight.

"I should've stayed," I whispered.

"You were outnumbered," Ben stated. "You did the
only thing you could."

"Pretty words," I mumbled. "Doesn't make me feel
any better."

The motor purred. Ben's slender fingers gripped the
steering wheel. "Where to?"

"Back to that shack."

He pulled onto Highway 16. I instructed him where to
go, and when he turned on the dirt road, he drove at a
snail's pace. The sky was light with dawn, but Ben loved
this car. He treated it like a princess. We crept over the
bumps that Dusty had flown over earlier.

"Why didn't you bring your Jeep?" I asked.

"I didn't think we were going off-road," Ben replied.

When we finally reached the shack, my heart jumped
in my throat. All three vehicles (Jack's, Dusty's and
Kate's) were gone. We got out, and I rushed to follow
the tracks. Unfortunately, they led straight into the Amite

River, but there wasn't any sign of the trucks or the Mustang.

As I stared at the river, Ben stepped up beside me. He held his weapon of choice in his left hand, balancing the butt of the tranquilizer CO2 rifle on his left hip. The darts were filled with the same stuff my bullets had – holy water.

Frustrated, I stomped back to the shack with Ben and Pete right behind me. Gun out, I climbed the rickety porch stairs and pushed open the creaky door. I hesitated, and a quick scan of the room assured me that it was empty. Still, my step remained cautious as I entered. The rest of the house proved unoccupied as well.

"Demon wings," I said.

"Where the hell are they?" Pete snapped and kicked a can across the small living room.

"Million dollar question," Ben responded as he began inspecting the contents of the shack. Of course, there wasn't much to inspect.

Taking his lead, I noticed several dilapidated pictures hanging on the walls in every room. Grime covered the glass on all, and I swiped my hand across several to reveal various swamp scenes with cypress trees, alligators and other dangerous wildlife. Apparently, the pictures weren't valuable as they'd been left to rot with the shack.

"I don't see any symbols drawn anywhere," Ben said.

"The place stinks of dead vampires," Pete growled, "but other than that, I can't find anything."

I kicked a wall and began to pace.

Ben pulled the spatula out of my back pocket. He twirled it in his hands. "Are you planning on cooking for us?"

I snatched it back. "Nope. I'm planning to call Jeneen so she can use this to scry for Jack."

***

Jeneen's House
Walker, LA
Thursday, December 28th, 10:00 AM
Countdown: 4 Days 5 Hours 59 Minutes 59 Seconds

"I am not touching that," Jeneen said with disgust.

She looked at me as if I were out of my mind. I held the egg-encrusted spatula across the kitchen table between us. My eyes locked with hers, but I refused to back down.

"Not even with rubber gloves?" I asked.

She wrinkled her nose. "My skin has to touch the object for scrying to work, and that has Hell stink on it."

My friend sat back and crossed her arms. Her shoulder length, brown hair was pulled up in a ponytail, and her pajamas were Christmas red satin.

"I'm a pure witch, Angelle. I don't deal in dark magic, and that *thing* is covered in it."

I crossed my arms and tapped my foot. "Remember how I saved your grimoire from the fire demon?"

Her face paled, and her shoulders sagged a little. Her determined face softened. "Yeah."

"I'm cashing in my *owe you one*."

Sighing, she held out her palm. "I still have the spell I used when my dog tangled with that skunk."

I quickly dropped the spatula into her hand before she changed her mind. She jiggled it around while watching me closely. Ben sat to my left, drumming his fingers on the table, and Pete sat on my right, tapping his foot.

"Don't stress so much. We will find them," Jeneen said.

She tied a long string to the hole at the end of the spatula and dangled it over a map spread out on the table. The spatula swung in a wide circle. She gave me a doubtful glance. "Crystal works best for scrying."

151

"Not for residents of Hell," I said.

The spatula mesmerized me as it swung in a circle. It started out fast and slowed to a lazy spin. Suddenly, it dropped to the table as if a magnet had pulled it down. Jeneen and I leaned close. The spatula landed on the Amite River, covering a two inch stretch of land north of my bar. While the scrying indicated a large area, I already knew where to go.

"The shack," I whispered. "But we searched that place and found zilch."

The spatula rose up slowly, defying gravity, and stood straight up in the air. The cooking utensil remained there unwavering.

I looked past it at Jeneen's face. Her eyes were wide, and her mouth had formed an 'o'. She snatched her hand away from the string. The spatula hung for a second by itself before collapsing into a heap on the map.

"How'd you do that?" I asked.

"I didn't." Her voice cracked with fear. She pointed a shaky finger toward the table. "Please, remove it from my sight."

I did as she asked while she jumped up and ran to the kitchen sink. She turned on the water and scrubbed the Hell out of her hands … literally. She dried them and held her nose to her fingertips. She repeated this process about five times before satisfied.

"That's worse than trying to get rid of the smell of catfish from your hands," she grumbled.

"Why did that happen?" Ben asked.

Jeneen stayed by the sink and rested her back against the counter. She crossed her arms and lifted her shoulders briefly. "I don't know."

"So where does this leave us?" Pete asked.

"Back to the shack," I replied. "Maybe it's a portal, and we missed the door."

A light bulb went off in my head, and I dug the owl key out of my back pocket. I held it up. "Did ya'll see any odd shaped keyholes on the doors?"

Ben and Pete shook their heads. Jeneen took the key and examined it. She tossed it back to me and said, "I don't know what that would fit, but if you want me to go with you, I guess I can work past my *issues*."

"No. I don't need one more friend in danger of getting kidnapped."

My stomach rumbled, reminding me the last time I ate had been over twelve hours ago. The rest of my body decided to chime in and protest of weariness. My arms were suddenly heavy, and a slight headache began behind my eyes. I yawned and shook my head, trying to keep my eyes open.

"Would you please make some coffee?" I asked.

Jeneen nodded, getting up from the table. "Are you hungry? I have some cereal bars."

"Yes," responded the three of us at the same time.

She opened a cabinet, reached in and pulled out three tiny packages. She tossed them to us and proceeded to fix a pot of coffee.

Ben picked up a pen and circled the area where the shack was located. Then he circled the areas where my house and the bar were located. He drew a line connecting all the bubbles. "Well, unless a backwards seven is the new Bermuda Triangle or demonic symbol, that experiment was a bust."

I shrugged, fighting back another yawn. "Doesn't hurt to explore all possibilities."

Jeneen set the pot of coffee on the table and a plate full of cookies. We set upon the food and drink like starved dogs, discussing the situation between bites.

"Trina said that their mother wants a word with me," I said. Clasping my hands around the mug of coffee, I stared into the mocha colored liquid. "I don't know who their mother is, but I have a feeling she and I have met before."

As Jeneen re-took her seat across from me, I yawned again. She arched an eyebrow. "Do I bore you?"

I shook my head. "Guess it's all just catching up with me. I haven't slept in over twenty four hours."

"May I offer a suggestion then?" the white witch asked.

Taking a sip of coffee, I nodded. "Sure."

"Your first course of action needs to be rest. You can't fight this bitch and her minions on caffeine alone."

Ben snorted. "Says you."

"We need to act while the sun is up," Pete said. Angry anxiety laced his words.

I chewed my lower lip. "You both have a solid point. So we compromise. The only problem is that I can't go home to take a nap. I'm positive they have the house staked out with human minions."

"You can crash in my spare room," Jeneen offered.

"Are you sure? I'm a filthy mess." I picked a stray piece of branch out of my hair.

"Sheets wash. Don't worry about it."

I pushed back from the table and looked at Pete. "Thank you so much. Ben, make sure I'm up by 2 pm."

Jeneen led me to the bedroom, and I gave her a brief hug and said, "Thanks for opening up your house to us."

"You're welcome," she replied and shut the door, giving me privacy.

Peeling off my filthy shirt and jeans, I climbed into bed wearing just my bra and undies before I pulled the covers over me. Holding up the owl key, I stared intently at it.

When it became obvious the inanimate object wouldn't give up its secrets, I let out a sigh of frustration. Of course, I hadn't really expected it to start talking, but in my weird world, anything was possible.

I leaned back, and the minute my head hit the pillow, I was out like an angel light.

***

CHAPTER 16

The Shack by Amite River
Watson, LA
Thursday, December 28th, 3:30 PM
Countdown: 4 Days 0 Hours 29 Minutes 59 Seconds

"How do we know what to look for?" Pete asked.

I stood at the bottom of the shack's rickety porch steps. My Walther PPK was ready to take on any vampire (born or sired) that got in my way. The bullets wouldn't completely destroy them, but it would slow them down. Ben led the way with his trusty tranquilizer gun, and Pete brought up the rear with an axe.

"We don't know. It's trial and error," I said. "If the plan even works."

I had woken with a clearer head and an idea of what to do next. So with a stomach full of Jeneen's leftover lasagna, the three of us had headed back to the shack.

"The owl key has to open the portal," I told them.

Trouble was, the portal could be in the shape of anything. While typical doors are large and square, some run from the size of a pebble to a small lake. A portion of the Amite River could be the one or some inanimate object in the shack. The only way to find out was for the key to touch the portal door.

So I commenced to pressing the owl key against everything in the shack, starting with the steps. Ben made sure each room was clear before we entered.

Before long, we went in to the room where I'd found Marishka.

Glass shards from the busted window littered the floor. My boots crunched them as I continued my exploration with the key. The last area to check was the closet.

I pulled open the door to reveal a large picture of a cypress tree. I'd seen it on an earlier visit but had thought nothing of it. Now, I had other ideas. Bracing myself for the effects of a portal opening, I pressed the owl key to the painting.

Nothing happened.

My shoulders sagged as I stepped back. "Well, that was a bust."

"Maybe you have to touch it at a certain place," Ben suggested. "Not just randomly."

I studied the painting. The cypress knees, which grew from the tree roots and protruded out of the water, surrounded the tree like a court protecting its queen. The tree sat in the middle of a swamp, and an alligator's head floated in the distance. The yellow eye seemed to look directly at me, and I quickly looked back at the tree.

Moss hung from its branches, and an owl hid within the gray mass. I immediately pressed the key to the owl. *A perfect fit.*

I let go, and the key remained attached to the painting. Other than that, nothing changed. I glanced quizzically at Ben, who shrugged.

"Beats me," he said.

I pulled the key from the painting, and a loud groaning ensued from the tree. All three of us jumped back as the painting came to life. The alligator swam towards us.

The cypress knees crawled out of the painting and spread throughout the room. Typically, the width of cypress knees could reach about two feet at the most. The ones forming around us had widths from two to five foot, which meant the growing cypress tree had to be the king of all trees. While the knees were pointed, they tops were wide enough for me to place a foot on each one as red water seeped out and covered the floor. Ben and Pete did the same. A metallic stench filled the air as the dark water covered my boots. I dipped my finger into the thick water. It had to be blood, but I wasn't about to taste it to find out.

The base of the tree grew out of the painting and filled up the closet. Miraculously, the house did not fall apart. It simply faded as the portal overtook the room.

"What now, genius?" Pete asked as he balanced on two cypress knees.

"I'm thinking," I replied.

"Well speed up your thinking. We have company coming," Ben stated and pointed at the alligator.

Swimming was out of the question. There were too many alligators, garfish and other icky predators to content with. Plus, I had no desire to immerse myself in what had to be dark magic blood.

"Let's climb onto the tree to get a better view," I said, pocketing the owl key.

"I don't think that's a good idea," Pete said, pointing.

On every limb sat four or five owls, ranging from babies to old birds. Every single one regarded us intently with their gold-flecked brown eyes, and as if on cue, they all started hooting eerily and stretching their wings.

Normal owls are creepy enough, especially when they spin their heads like the chick in The Exorcist. These owls didn't qualify as normal. The main weirdness stemmed from their size. The babies were the size of a Labrador retriever, and the adults the size of horses. My instincts screamed at me to run away from the owls, but when have I ever listened to any good advice?

"There might be enough room inside the hollow part of the trunk for us to get in," Ben suggested.

"And do what?" Pete snapped. "Invite all the woodland animals in for a tea party?"

"Ya'll, please chill," I said as I forced myself to use the cypress knees to get closer to the owl-infested tree. Wrapped around it was a rope the same color as the tree.

This cypress had to be the largest I'd ever seen. The width of its base equaled a ten by ten bedroom, and the top of it reached up into the clouds. At first, I thought we'd have to climb it. The bark felt hard and dry beneath my fingertips. I peered into the open center of the tree, hoping to find something ... a door ... or even Jack. Unfortunately, it held nothing. I shimmied around the base using the knees as stepping stones and found the rope tied to a small flat-bottomed boat known as a bateau.

I smiled. "Jackpot."

Ben and Pete were right behind me, and we all clamored in to the boat. Ben cranked on the 5H motor several times before it purred to life.

He laughed. "Where to, captain?"

I surveyed the area. "We need to remember where this tree is so we can get home."

"It's the tallest one around," Pete stated. "We can probably see it from anywhere."

Carefully, I grabbed a handful of Spanish moss from one of the low limbs. "Jeneen taught me a tracking spell that is super easy."

I dropped the moss into the bottom of the boat, and just as I thought it strange that the bateau had been left unguarded, an alligator the size of a tugboat floated to the surface.

The good news was that the beast was on the other side of the prehistoric cypress tree.

The bad news was the beast was just on the other side of the prehistoric cypress. His huge head poked out from the right side while his enormous tail curled from the left. Fortunately, the front of the bateau was pointed toward the tail.

"Um, Ben, I think you need to gun it," I said.

Unfortunately, the motor only pushed us about four miles per hour – not fast enough to get away from the monster-gator. I watched behind us as it swished around the cypress tree and came after us.

"Um, Ben, can you make this thing go faster?" I asked and bit my lower lip.

"Only if you have a bigger motor on ya," he responded.

"I can run faster than this," Pete said. A low growl rolled out of his mouth as the gator quickly caught up with us. The beast opened its jaws, and water dripped from teeth the length of Pete's arm.

"This isn't working," I hollered.

"Hold on," Ben yelled, and just as I grabbed the side of the boat, he jerked it to the right.

Jaws smashed down on the water beside us.

Ben headed the boat toward a grove of cypress trees. The beast continued after us.

The sun was still up but about to set. The trees laid shadows all over the swamp. When we got closer to the grove, the shadows crawled out from the trees, creating a dark mist over the water that enveloped us in its embrace.

The gator slid to a stop beside us, creating four foot waves. I held on tight as the bateau rocked precariously. Fortunately, the beast couldn't see us because of Ben's cloaking ability.

The dino-gator's growl rumbled like thunder around the bayou and sent fear racing down my spine.

Ben cut off the motor, and we drifted with the current, which went the opposite direction of where the gigantic alligator swam. All of us froze in our spots and watched him as he turned his head left and right, searching in vain for his prey – us.

He slapped his tail against the water, sent out another angry growl and swam back to the cypress tree he guarded.

I let out the breath I'd been holding. "Thank you, Ben."

"My pleasure."

Ben started the motor and eased us down the bayou and away from the monster-gator.

"Where are we going?" he asked.

I lifted my hands in an "I don't know" gesture. "I guess we'll know it when we see it."

The motor hummed as we putted along the bayou. A white crane swooped in front of us as it headed for a grove of cypress trees to our right. The bird landed in shallow water and froze with its neck stretched out. It stepped slowly forward, but before I could see what the crane stalked, the boat had moved so that a tree blocked my view.

I focused on the area we headed toward. The dark water stretched out like a road between the groves of cypress trees. Several birds cawed from above, flying from the top of one tree to another. The swamp's surface beauty masked the hidden danger. Below the water swam gators, snakes, garfish and much more. I had no desire to tangle with those predators today, especially in this alternate reality that began to resemble a dinosaur movie.

We rounded the bend, and the bayou opened up into a vast lake. About a half a mile from us, there was a point of land that widened into an island covered in brush and tall, thin cypress trees.

"Let's check it out," I said.

Ben eased us to the edge of land, and Pete jumped out, tied the boat to a cypress tree and helped me out. The soft ground squished as I walked over it. The cold air forced me to pull up the collar on my jacket. I stuck my hands in the pockets and studied the bayou behind us as

Ben got out of the boat. The blood-colored water rushed silently past, carrying dead tree limbs and other debris.

We trudged deeper into the woods. Trying to avoid stepping on crunchy leaves and limbs was like trying to avoid taking a breath of air. I did the best I could, but I was envious of how easily the Werewolf made it look. Pete's heavy foot made no sound in the woods, though I recalled how loud his walk on the bar's wooden front porch could be.

Lights flickered in the distance, and laughter cackled on the breeze. The air danced with more voices, and the closer we got, the more worried I became.

We stopped, and placing my hands against the cold bark of a tree, I peered around it and froze.

A two story plantation sat on a hill in the middle of the swamp. The front yard consisted of knee high grass that crawled up the stone steps. Fancy columns dotted the front porch, and railings lined the second floor balcony.

Twenty vampires stood on its porch. A few dined on catatonic humans who were sitting in various chairs. More roamed inside the house, and I could see their figures as they moved by open windows. They were all female, and they all looked like Trina.

***

Swamp
Alternate Reality
Thursday, December 28th, 4:00 PM
Countdown: 3 Days 23 Hours 59 Minutes 59 Seconds

The King James version of Isaiah 34:13 reads "And thorns shall come up in her palaces, nettles and brambles in the fortresses thereof: and it shall be a habitation of dragons, and a court for owls."

The plantation qualified as a palace, which is what made me think of the bible verse. Spanish moss covered the roof, and humungous cypress trees surrounded the plantation. Thousands of owls perched in the moss and anywhere else they could find a ledge. Snakes slithered around the limbs of the cypress trees, and alligators sunbathed on the lawn surrounding the plantation.

I remembered reading somewhere that dinosaurs were sometimes called dragons. Alligators are smaller versions of the Deinosuchus, their dinosaur counterpart. These ancient monsters weighed up to 8.5 tons and were as long as 39 feet. The gigantic alligator guarding the cypress tree had to be a Deinosuchus.

The owl key in my pocket had I3413 inscribed on the back of it, further connecting it to the scripture and the *her* it spoke of. I began to have an inkling as to the *her* who was at the bottom of all this, but just as I was about to voice my idea to Ben and Pete, two of the metaphorical dragons appeared – one to our right and one on our left.

Effectively trapping us against the tree, the two gators growled and hissed at us but didn't charge. Just as I aimed the PPK at one of the beasts, another gator appeared in front of us, snapping its jaws, grunting and growling. I shifted my gun to this one, but something made me hesitate.

The gator equaled the length of my motorbike, and white tufts of hair sprouted from the top of its head. Alligators don't have hair, but while my mind tried to wrap around the anomaly, the tufts lengthened. In fact, the head of the gator shifted into the head of a man and continued until the upper portion had arms and a torso. The bottom part remained gator, and the Were stood on its hind legs.

"You're trespassing." His gritty voice matched his roughened, tan skin. His eyes swirled gator-black with shades of mossy green, and he had them focused on me.

One of his eye teeth remained that of a gator's and extended out of his mouth eerily.

I held my hands open, trying to show respect. "We are only here to find our friends. We don't want any trouble."

"Too bad. You found it," he snapped.

A tall lady stepped from behind a cypress tree. Her flowing white hair hung to her knees, covering her naked body. Her skin was tanned, and the wrinkles on her face weren't enough to mar her beauty. She placed her left hand on the Were-gator's arm. "Bob, maybe we should let them go. I've had a vision of her."

She pointed at me with her right hand. I narrowed my eyes, wondering if it were a good or bad vision.

The were-gator shrugged her hand away. "Get thee back to the nest, woman. This here is business. Our Queen--"

"Ha," the lady grunted. "Queen my tail … she's got you wrapped around her finger, Bob. What has she done to you?"

He faced her and leaned close to her. "Not a damn thing I didn't want done. Now get."

The lady lifted her chin and slipped back into the woods. The were-gator turned back to us and crossed his arms. "Now, where were we? Oh yes, I was about to feed you to my clan."

Pete took one step forward. His right hand shifted into wolf. He raised it in a non-threatening manner. "Brother, I ask you let us pass in peace."

The old-gator man hissed and snapped his mouth open and shut as if he were still in complete alligator form. "You're not my Brother, and my Queen's orders are that none shall trespass on her land and live to tell the tale."

Shifting into full gator-mode, he rushed at Pete, who only had time to side step. He took a swipe at the old gator, and the Werewolf's claws scraped down scaly hide.

The gator closest to me growled and started crawling toward me, drawing my attention away from Pete's battle. Without hesitation, I shot the gator right between the eyes, and it slid to a stop at my feet, dead on arrival.

Ben shot a tranquilizer into the gator that attacked him, but the liquid inside did nothing to stop the beast. It kept going, and Ben swerved to avoid it just in the nick of time.

Alligators suddenly appeared all around us, and it was every fallen angel, vampire and Werewolf for themselves. I cleared a path by shooting the ones closest to me, and I ran. When I reached a safe area, I turned around, but Ben and Pete were nowhere to be found. We had been effectively separated, and I knew we had played right in to *the mother's* hands.

"Dancing demon wings," I muttered.

Gathering my bearings, I slipped through the woods and found my way back to the plantation. Hiding behind a tree, I realized that I had come upon the side of the plantation. As on the front, columns held up the second floor balcony. The shutters to all the windows were either missing or hanging from their hinges. Foliage from the woods grew right up to the house, and there weren't any vampires or humans around. It struck me as odd that this side wasn't guarded.

Just as that thought entered my head, the foliage moved like waves on the ocean. Something patrolled this side, and I backed up, unwilling to find out what kind of monster it was. I had no desire to fight a Volkswagen-sized spider or a python the size of a train. My skin crawled at the mere thought.

A human stepped onto the upper balcony, and a vampire followed behind her. Around the human's throat was a collar with a leash attached to it, which the vampire held. The human's face had morphed into half-weredog, and rage rose in my throat as I realized it was Kate.

The foliage continued to wave as its guard played sentinel beneath it. I reloaded my gun and pulled out the knife in my boot. It seemed I had a monster to slay.

The minute I stepped into the dense foliage, something slipped around my ankle, and I glanced down, expecting to see a spider's hairy leg. I was wrong. A piece of magic rope yanked my foot out from under me and pulled me into the air. A holler slipped from my lips, and I cringed as it echoed around the trees.

Swinging upside down, my long hair touched the ground. I pulled myself up and my fingers pried at the rope, but the magic wasn't letting go of me.

I expected vampires to swarm me. However, only one person approached. I tilted my head, trying to clarify who I thought it was. My heart filled with joy at the sight of Jack's smiling face.

***

CHAPTER 17

Swamp
Alternate Reality
Thursday, December 28th, 4:30 PM
Countdown: 3 Days 23 Hours 29 Minutes 59 Seconds

I waved my arms wildly at him. "Help me down before they get here."

He remained silent and strolled toward me. When his face became level with mine, he placed his hands on my cheeks and sniffed my face. Before I could wonder about his strange behavior, he rubbed my hair against his cheek and pressed his lips to mine. He stole my breath, and as he stepped away, I gasped for air.

Jack's mouth twisted into a half-smile, and his hooded eyes sent fear through me. "You taste like an angel … and you smell like an angel."

"Yeah, and I'm pissed like an angel, too." Gravity pulled at my arms, but I kept them crossed over my chest as my body swung helpless. "Can you get me down? Kinda got some baddies lurking around, and we'll never escape at this rate."

The light in Jack's eyes glittered with blood, and fear pierced my heart and caught my breath. He placed two fingers over my lips. Looking over his shoulder, I noticed the two short vampires standing behind him. They reminded me of groupies, and I frowned as Jack faced them.

"Cut the rope from the tree and get her down," he ordered, "but don't take it off her ankle."

Terror filled my throat with cotton. "Jack? What are you doing? We need to get out of here. We can take these two. Jack?"

He turned back to me, and the blood-colored eyes scared me to the core. Where was the blue?

I forced myself not to panic. One of his groupies cut the rope from the tree with a magic enhanced knife, and Jack caught me before I hit the ground. I tried to repress a shudder as he hugged me to him and walked toward the house.

"I've missed you," he whispered. "Wish I could keep you longer but ... well ... my Queen has plans for you."

As he placed a foot on the steps leading up to the porch, I came to life and kicked my legs. I caught him off balance, and he stumbled back, missed a step and was forced to let go of me as we tumbled down. Jumping to my feet, I started running.

I didn't get far. The rope around my ankle pulled tight and tripped me. I landed with an *oof*, and Jack immediately dragged me through the muck and mud. He flipped me onto my back and straddled me with his knees on either side of my arms. I bucked wildly. His left hand circled my throat and held me firmly in place.

"How are you stronger than me? Tell me the truth, Jack." I licked my lips and regretted it. I spit gritty mud into his face and waited for a resounding slap, but he merely lifted his hand and swiped it off. "You're a blood addict, aren't you?"

His cold smile revealed nothing, and his icy eyes remained red instead of blue. "Now is not the time for questions. Be a good girl."

He stood, flung me over his shoulder and began walking again. Ever the fighter, I pulled my upper body straight up ... in time to crack my head on the roof of the porch. White pain blasted through the back of my head, and I fell back across his shoulder.

"I said be good. That's what you get for not listening." His deep voice rumbled in his chest.

"When have I ever?" I mumbled against his black t-shirt.

"Never," he chuckled. "And that's what I was counting on."

"Where are you taking me?" My stomach bounced against his shoulder.

"You'll see."

I flung my hands out, grabbing at things as we passed by. I had to get away. This did not bode well. As we passed a set of stairs, I grabbed the railing. It stopped him short. Patiently, he backed up and extricated my hand finger by finger.

"Let me go, Jack. Please."

Ignoring me, he continued down the hall. I continued grabbing at things and managed to get hold of a tall, wooden floor candle. Inhaling a deep breath, I gathered up my strength and pulled my upper body up. With the base of the candle holder, I cracked him on the back of the head. Blood oozed out of the cut and into his hair.

He didn't drop me, but he did stop walking. His jaw clenched as he wrenched the weapon out of my hand and threw it across the hall. A female vampire yelped as it hit her. I looked down into his face, but he wasn't mad.

Setting me on my feet, he grasped my left hand firmly in his. He made me walk beside him, and I dug my heels in. I wasn't about to make it easy simply because he was winning. He yanked on me forward.

"Give it up, woman," he muttered.

"Never."

The blood, which had rushed to my head earlier, swooped back down, and a woozy feeling slammed into me. My stomach churned and bubbled. I'd read somewhere vomit was a good defensive tactic. Attackers were usually turned off by it. Oh wait … that was rapists not kidnappers.

Before I could stick my finger down my throat to try, he stopped in front of a door and looked me over. He ran his hands over my hair, fixing the mess, and he tugged my muddy shirt down over my exposed belly. He knocked on the door.

"*Entreveaux*," a female voice tinkled on the other side of the door. Jack pushed it open and indicated for me to go first.

"You're such a gentleman," I said. My lip curled up in agitation as I passed by him. He followed and shut the door behind us.

Opulence covered the room from one corner to the next. Several elegant lounging couches accommodated vampires with their human pets. Food for the victims sat atop ornately carved wooden coffee tables. Along the walls, china cabinets held various knickknacks such as a Native American headdress and a curved saber that rested atop a Confederate solder's uniform. I assumed these were tokens of their conquests.

On the other side of the room sat two high-backed chairs, which resembled thrones. Trina reclined in one … or what appeared to be her. An exquisite purple lily rested behind her right ear. Her purple and black dress reminded me of the Queen of Hearts, and its hem reached the floor while her bodice pushed her bosom up and out. Her beauty surpassed the other vampires roaming the plantation.

I stopped in the middle of the room, reluctant to approach her. If I was her next meal, Jack would have to drag me kicking and screaming.

He placed a hand on my shoulder and forced me to my knees. "See, my queen? I told you she'd come here of her own free will."

"No, I'm not." I almost bit my tongue in my haste. "I'm not here of my own free will, not anymore. So whatever you've got planned, it's not going to work if I'm not willing to do it."

Head held high and chin higher, the woman stood. With her shoulders back and chest pushed out, she sashayed over to us. I had to admit she had an air of majesty around her. She took my chin in her hand and pity filled her eyes.

"Does not matter." Her words were crisp and clear with a slight Hungarian accent. "That you came here for Jack and your friends ... sacrificed yourself for them, so to speak ... of your own free will ... is what brought you through my door, and that is all we needed."

Before I could protest, she stepped beside me and pulled my muddy shirt up, inspecting my back. Jack held me firmly as her hands traced the two scars near my shoulder blades. The memory surfaced of when my wings were ripped away, and I swore I could actually feel the pain again. The woman dropped my shirt and walked around us until she stood in front of me again. She grabbed my hands and smelled my wrists.

"Ah ... angel blood ... I have not dined on that in centuries."

I stared at her beautiful face as some distant memory nagged at me. She caught me staring and smiled. "Yes, we have met before. You would have known me then as Lilith."

***

Swamp
Alternate Reality
Thursday, December 28th, 5:00 PM
Countdown: 3 Days 22 Hours 59 Minutes 59 Seconds

A light bulb went off in my head, and hope briefly flitted through me. Lilith was the mother, a historical figure and the woman scorned.

Lilith had been Adam's first wife, and where Adam had been created of the purest of dust, Lilith had been made out of the foulest mud and dirt on earth. Nonetheless, she had believed herself his equal, if not better than him. In her eyes, he had treated her little better than a servant, and she finally fled the Garden of Eden. She went to the Red Sea, where she cavorted with demons. Obviously, she still copulated with them as evidenced by the presence of her daughters, known as the *liliam*. She had never born a son, proof she had control of the birthing process.

"So how's Eve? Seen her lately?" I asked flippantly.

Lilith's fingernails dug into my wrists, and she actually gnashed her teeth. "How is Lucifer? Oh wait … you escaped … much as I did. Congratulations."

"What do you want from me, Lilith? Come on. Spill your evil plan already," I said with a bit of impatience.

Letting go of me, she retraced her steps and sat on her cushioned throne. Crossing her arms, she inspected her freshly polished nails. "Tell me, Angelle. Do you like my home?"

I looked around her lavish *throne* room. Her daughters lounged around on red plush settees, high back cushioned chairs and pillows the size of dining tables. The *liliam* ate fruit, drank wine and fed off a few catatonic humans.

"Too much trash around for my taste," I replied. Jack dug his fingers in my shoulder, and I winced.

"Oh, I am so sad you do not like it," she purred. "I have worked hard on it over the past hundred and thirty five years that I have been stuck here."

"It's not the prison. It's the occupants. Seems you aren't lacking for male companionship … especially those demons you so love to screw. I must admit, your daughters are beautiful … even if they do have a bite to them."

She beamed. "Thank you. They are a mother's pride and joy."

"So what'd you do to land yourself in such a … pleasant prison?" I asked.

Lilith shrugged and frowned. "Angered a voodoo princess. Seems she was jealous and extremely upset that I took her man." She waved her hand. "But how I got here is of no importance. 'Tis how I am getting out that means the world to me, and I am glad that the last ingredient, you of course, has arrived."

I swallowed over the sudden lump in my throat. I had a funny feeling I wasn't going to like her escape plan. "So glad I could help with your recipe, Lilith, but I'm not much of a cook."

In an attempt to escape from Jack's grip, I dipped my right shoulder. His fingers dug in tighter, and I twisted left. His other hand caught my left shoulder, and he hauled me roughly to my feet.

"Where do you think you're going?" He chuckled.

"Home." The word sounded weak, even to my ears.

"Have patience, Angelle. I will send you home soon … just not your earthly one." Lilith's voice raised the hairs on my neck. "Upon ringing in the New Year, you, my lovely fallen angel, will be sacrificed for my freedom."

"I can't die." I tried not to think about my tattoo.

"Who said anything about dying?"

The blood slipped out of my face, and I couldn't breathe for a second. "You're giving me to Nate for your freedom? You can't do that. It's against my free will." My hollow words reflected the emptiness in my chest.

Lilith chortled. "Hence the reason you had to come after Jack, my dear. It was an *act* of free will, which is all I needed for the spell."

My shoulders slumped as fear of Hell rose inside me. I stared uneasily at Jack's shirt. Nate would get his way, and I'd be under his control again. This time, I wouldn't even have my angelic powers to fight him. I'd be going down there as a human. My hands shook.

"Take her to her room, Jack, and make her comfortable."

"Yes, my queen," he responded compliantly.

The second he let go of my shoulders, I threw an upper punch that took him by surprise. He hesitated, and I spun around, took a few steps back before running at him. I jumped and kicked him in the chest. The force threw him across the room and against the wall.

I turned to Lilith with a wicked smile. It was my kick-butt grin, and I assumed a fighting stance. "Time for me to knock that flower out of your hair."

She eyed me with a sudden twinkle in her eye and waved her hands regally from the top of her head to her waist. Her clothes changed to an expensive looking purple jogging suit. The lily remained tucked behind her ear.

"So, Lilith, has anyone ever told you how much of a slut you are?" I goaded.

Lilith sprang forward and struck me with her fist. If anyone could fight elegantly, it'd be Lilith. The way she moved and her small stature reminded me of a ballerina in a production of *West Side Story.* The only difference - her punches connected, and I took a blow on the chin. I shook my head and hit her face and then her stomach.

I swung my left leg around and connected with her jaw. I continued around in a circle, and seeing I had rung her bell a bit, I really went after Lilith.

My left fist hit her square in the cheek, but my right punch landed against her right shoulder. She lost her balance and stumbled back a few steps. I moved forward and continued the attack.

"So Lilith … how's it feel to know you *could have been* the mother of the human race?" I asked between gasping for air.

Her smooth forehead wrinkled slightly for the first time since my arrival. Her lips pulled back, revealing her little fangs. "Humph, at least I won't be blamed for eating forbidden fruit."

Lilith lunged at me, and as she reached for my throat, I grabbed her shoulders and threw her to my right. Her fingernails scratched my neck, but she stumbled away. I twirled around, not wanting to keep my back to her for one second. I kept my fists up, ready for her next attack. She jumped up and down on her toes, clearly ready for more.

"Tsk tsk, Lilith. You should know better than to let your anger get the best of you during a fight," I chided.

Her black hair fanned out as she spun to face me. "Nothing gets the best of me."

She came at me fast, and for the next several minutes, there wasn't time for witty jabs ... only physical. I matched Lilith blow-for-blow, but while I began to tire, she still looked fresh from a nap.

My breath came in short gasps, and my arms felt like lead. *How long had we been fighting?* Pride urged me to keep tossing punches.

Stepping forward, I went to kick her. She grabbed my foot and twisted so hard that it popped at the knee, and I crumpled to the floor. I bit back the holler of pain that wanted to erupt from my mouth, mad that I was down and out of the fight.

Lilith waved her hand at Jack. "Do you think you can manage her now?"

***

CHAPTER 18

Lilith's Plantation
Alternate Reality
Thursday, December 28th, 6:00 PM
Countdown: 3 Days 21 Hours 59 Minutes 59 Seconds

Jack scooped me in his arms, and I tried to kick myself free. He pinned me against his chest with little effort. My arms were trapped as well. He carried me through the plantation to a bedroom and laid me down on the soft bed.

"Jack." My voice cracked. "What's wrong with you? Why are you acting like this when vampires killed your parents?"

He sat beside me, and his cold smile pierced my heart. Then he pulled down his lower lip. Two red vampire holes stood out against the pink of his mouth. He crossed his arms and looked condescendingly at me.

"So now you know I'm not a blood addict." He leaned close to me. "But guess what? Trina's finishing my transformation tonight, and my queen said I can make you *my* blood addict if only for a short time."

He reached behind his back before slamming a syringe needle into my arm. The drug hit me fast and hard, but I was grateful. It dulled the pain of betrayal winding around my heart.

Unable to look at him, I turned my head to the left as a tear slid down. *Good Lord, when had I become such a weepy girl? Oh, yeah. When I met Jack. Damn that night.*

I should've kicked him out of my bar. His fingers warmed my chin as he forced me to look at him. His eyes had turned back to blue, and he wiped away the tear. Angrily, I pushed his hand back. "Leave me alone."

"It'll be okay," he whispered and stared intently into my eyes.

Here we go again. His demeanor had again taken a three hundred and sixty degree turn. One minute, he was Mr. Baddie and taking me to his queen. The next, he treated me like a lover. My heart couldn't take the knives he stabbed in it.

"What is with you?" I snapped. "Just go away and serve your Lilith. I guess your mother died in vain."

He pulled back from me as the coldness fell over him like a blanket of snow. He gulped loudly one time before turning to one of his groupies. Reaching out with his left hand, he pulled her against him. With his eyes still locked with mine, he planted a kiss on her pouty lips. The sight hurt more than any of Nate's cleverly crafted tortures, and Jack knew it.

As she sank into his spell, he carefully pushed her away. It didn't bother her. She simply stepped closer to me.

"I want to see the angel's wings."

"She's no longer an angel. She has no wings and never will again." Jack's words sliced through my heart.

Another vampire came in with an IV and drip bag. Unable to move, I watched as she took my right arm and thumped it for a vein. She plunged in a needle and hooked me up like in a hospital.

"Wow … a vampire nurse." My words had started to slur, and cloud nine had picked me up. "Do they pay you in blood?"

"Sometimes," she murmured.

I'd been joking. "Guess you work the night shift, huh?"

Jack pushed the vampire away and inspected her work. He leaned close and pressed his mouth to my ear. Anger washed over me, but I couldn't move. I had no idea where his luscious mouth had been.

"Have faith, and maybe one day, I'll bring you to a glass Magnolia."

Why did he refer to his Christmas gift?

He straightened and plunked his finger lightly against the IV dripping into my arm. "Just make sure this keeps flowing. Don't worry, sweetheart, when you're my addict, you won't need these terrible needles."

Jack tilted his head to his right as he stared at me. His mouth sneered, but his eyes seemed to plead with me. "Sweet dreams, Angelle."

I assumed that the IV was filled with elephant tranquilizer. Jack's image blurred, and I blinked, struggling to remain coherent. My brows creased, and my tongue felt like cotton.

My eyelids closed, and I floated in a sea of darkness. In the distance, a small dot of light appeared, and I struggled toward it. The light took shape and appeared to be a door, but when I got closer, it became a mirror. Instead of my image, the reflection was of Lilith. She moved when I moved.

This was some hallucination from the drugs.

My hand pressed to the mirror, as did Lilith's, but instead of my palm meeting cold glass, flesh met flesh. Her hand slid out of the mirror, wrapped around my wrist and yanked me into her prison. I fell at her feet, but when I looked up at her, Lilith had been replaced by an old hag with dull gray hair.

Her bright green eyes flashed angrily, and she leaned her wrinkled face close to mine. Rancid breath fanned my nose, and I tried not to gag.

"I kicked your ass once," the hag snarled, "and I'll do it again."

Someone's hands slipped under my arms and hauled me to my feet. I looked over my shoulder, and Jack stared solemnly at me. Blood seeped from the corners of his eyes and trailed down his cheeks.

He pulled me into his arms and hugged me. I resisted at first, but the warmth of his embrace calmed my fears. I hugged him back, closing my eyes and burying my face in his shoulder.

My mouth filled with a tangy, tart taste, and my eyes flew open. My fingers were wrapped around a wrist, and my mouth was pressed to flesh. Warm metallic liquid filled my throat. The second realization set in, I stopped drinking and shoved Jack's arm away. I touched my fingers to my lips and looked at them. They were red with his blood.

My stomach clenched, and bile rose in my throat. I leaned over the bed just in time. Red liquid splashed all over the floor, his shoes and some of his jeans. I rolled onto my back and glared at him.

"You son of a bitch." My hand connected with his cheek, and the crack resonated through the room. The force of it would've snapped a normal man's neck. Jack smiled, revealing two pearly white fangs.

I checked my wrists for bite marks and ran my fingers over my neck. He chuckled. "Don't worry. You're not a vampire."

My stomach spiked with fear, and the color drained from my face. "What have you done?"

"What I promised I'd do."

I searched his eyes but couldn't find any remorse. "But you hate vampires."

"That was before I understood them."

My skin crawled, and a terrible thirst clawed at my stomach. My eyes closed, and I rolled onto my side, refusing to believe what was happening to me. I couldn't shake the desire hitting me. It was like I had eaten a bag of salty chips and needed a tall, icy glass of water. My new craving demanded something other than the normal human drink. It demanded more of Jack's sweet blood.

I wept as the reality of what he had done sunk in. "Oh my God."

He held his wrist under my nose. The open wound glared at me, and I turned my head in disgust at myself. He ruthlessly held me down and forced me to drink. Little pinpoints of fear prickled my body. Now I would be forever bound to a vampire if I wanted to live. They would control me and make my life a living hell. I was doomed.

I was a blood addict.

***

Bedroom
Alternate Reality
Saturday, December 30th, 9:00 PM
Countdown: 1 Days 18 Hours 59 Minutes 59 Seconds

I turned my head to the side as anger filled my heart. Jack's fingers slid under my chin, and he forced me to look at him.

"You will no longer feel the need to escape," he said.

The thoughts of doing that very thing had been swirling in the back of my mind, but while the idea remained, the want slipped away upon his command. My stomach twisted as fear sank in to the very core of my being.

"You will no longer fight me. You will willingly obey everything I tell you to do."

Pain and anger swirled in my heart, and I narrowed my eyes. "I thought we were friends. Guess I was wrong."

Speaking those words caused my heart to splinter into icy shards of glass. Jack faltered, and hurt dashed over his face so fast I knew I had to have mistaken it. His eyes hardened.

"You will speak only when spoken to."

My mouth opened to tell him what I thought of his *commands*, but the words in my throat sank back into my stomach. I still wanted to say them but couldn't and curled my fists around the blanket in frustration. Jack gulped, and my mouth half-grinned in short lived satisfaction. This wasn't easy for him. Good.

He left his perch on the side of the bed and went to the dresser. He carried a box of baby wipes over and proceeded to clean my face. "I'm sorry you can't have a proper bath. My queen won't allow water in the house."

The back of his warm hand hesitated against my cheek, and I battled the desire to sink into his touch. With a start, I realized I had been falling for him. He didn't deserve the tiny bud that could have been love but that was now buried beneath the rubble of my heart. I blinked back tears and concentrated on my anger.

After I was suitably cleaned up, he grabbed my hand and pulled me out of the bed. "My queen wants to talk to you."

The door creaked as he opened it, and he led me through the many hallways. I noted there were no mirrors. Instead of pictures, tapestry adorned the walls, and I didn't see any silver. So there was no water, no mirror, no silver and no glass.

I wondered if there was a kitchen and what kind of utensils there were, if any. Pots and pans would provide a reflection, but as vampires didn't eat normal food, I highly doubted the kitchen would be stocked for use.

Jack knocked on the door to the throne room, and we entered upon Lilith's bidding. He walked me right up to her chair and forced me to my knees. I had become a puppet on a string, and the anger caused my head to explode with a slight headache.

Jack parked his butt in the chair next to Lilith, and she whispered in his ear. I heard what she said and dreaded his next words. "You are to stop listening to words not meant for your ears."

Crap. No more eavesdropping. The world suddenly sounded less noisy.

Lilith leaned close to him again. Jack hesitated. "She wants to know if you've had ... sex since you've become human."

"No."

The word slipped out before I could even try to stop it. What did that info have to do with anything? It wasn't like they were sacrificing me ... hopefully. I'd thought it was gonna be more like a "Here ya go, Satan. This chick for my freedom" type of deal. Besides, truth be told, my soul wasn't virgin territory. Lilith knew I'd been head of the lust demons.

The self-proclaimed "queen" stared at me, but I refused to look down and focused on the purple lily in her hair. I was surprised she didn't tell Jack to make me look at her. Her gaze seemed more of curiosity than her usual pompousness.

"I am surprised Lucifer let you go." She tapped a polished nail against her mouth.

My escape from Hell had been amazingly easier than falling from Heaven.

She whispered in Jack's ear, and his eyes piqued with interest. He leaned forward, anxious for an answer. "She wants to know how you escaped."

Unwanted memories stumbled through a door in my mind. The horrors of Hell were too much to describe. "My escape had been organized by outside help. Michael had a huge hand in it."

She nodded. "Ah, yes. Mr. Archangel himself. How is the old coot?"

The thought suddenly occurred to me she could ask me the secret to my demise, and I'd give it to her as easily as spreading whipped butter on bread. Fear shot through me, and my body trembled.

"What makes you so special God broke you out of jail?" Her eyes narrowed.

Fortunately, I wasn't obligated to answer her questions, only Jack's. Good thing. I honestly didn't know why God was so amenable to me. I had to be one of the biggest sinners ever, and He wasn't big on letting fallen angels back into heaven.

Lilith whispered in Jack's ear, and I braced myself for the next round of truth or truth. The color drained from Jack's face, but he posed the question anyway. "Lilith would like to know how it feels to be betrayed by the one you love."

My heart twisted, and a tidal wave of pain engulfed me. "Hell feels better."

A shadow crossed her face. I was positive she was recalling her own lost first love. "That's putting it mildly," she muttered.

She patted Jack's hand. "Go. Take her to the dining room, and let her eat. One of my pets is grilling a steak for her."

My traitorous stomach grumbled, despite the tear that had slipped out and slid down my cheek. So much for my bad-ass reputation. The thought helped steel my resolve. No girly weeping. Turn the pain into anger, and let it fester.

Jack grabbed my hand and pulled me up. Our eyes met, and my chest felt as if it were filled with bricks. I looked away and stuck my chin up in the air. He sighed and pulled me along.

While I ate, silence weighed upon the dining room. My plastic fork scratched against the paper plate. He watched me eat every morsel as if he studied me for a quiz.

"Were you really falling in love with me?" Jack asked.

My heart exploded, and the pieces landed in my stomach. My traitorous lips readily answered him. "I think so."

Damn compulsion.

Anger welled up in me like an inflated balloon, but I had no outlet except in my head. My silent scream of frustration echoed in my skull.

My hands shook, and I dropped the plastic fork and knife. I managed to shove the plate of half-eaten steak away.

Jack pushed it back toward me. "Finish your food, Angelle. You'll need your strength."

Honest to God, I resisted obeying his command. My body, on the other hand, was a thing possessed. Despite the fact my appetite had long ago vanished, I devoured the rest of the steak.

I sat back and stared at the now-empty paper plate. Anger pounded through my blood, and I refused to focus on his handsome face. The desire to run from him should have been in the forefront, but as he had ordered me not to want that ...

"I ..." Jack started.

The air between us cracked with uncertainty. I crossed my arms and waited for his next command. His eyes stared intently at me, and I couldn't resist looking.

Big mistake number ... aw, hell, I'd lost count.

The blaze of lust in his eyes ignited a fire in me, and I wanted to throw the table out of the way to get to him. But whether it was to kill him or kiss him, I wasn't sure.

Damn it, girl, he's the enemy now. He doesn't care about you. He would never do this to someone he cares about.

"I wish I could make you understand." The lust in his eyes gave way to pain. He scooted his chair back. "Follow me. I want to show you around. Pay attention ... as I might need you to run errands around the house for me."

The house was a maze and huge beyond belief. We went through it at least twenty times, including the kitchen. Unfortunately, all the pots were made of cast iron, and not one stupid thing in the kitchen would cast a reflection.

Jack brought me back to his room, or rather, rooms. Not only did he have a bedroom, but he had a sitting room as well. He told me to take a seat on the small couch and relax. He sat on a nearby chair and smiled sheepishly.

"Gee … if I'd only had this power when I was a teenager."

His comment added flame to the fire, but I couldn't make a verbal reply. So I crossed my arms and stared at him. His smiled faded, and I hoped he realized what a stupid comment he'd made.

Someone knocked on the door. Jack hesitated and mouthed the words, *Trust me.*

"Come in," he said.

One of the groupies peeped in. "Lilith wants to see you both … now."

***

CHAPTER 19

Lilith's Court
Alternate Reality
Saturday, December 30th, 10:00 PM
Countdown: 1 Day 17 Hours 59 Minutes 59 Seconds

"Your friends have failed," said Lilith.

She peered down her nose at me as I knelt before her. "Jack, darling, did you feed her your blood?"

"She dined just before we left our room."

I glanced at him. *Why did he lie to her?*

"Perfect," Lilith purred. She snapped her fingers, and one of her daughters pushed in a cart. A brown, cardboard box the size of a nineteen inch TV sat on it. My eyes grew wide, and I think I stopped breathing. *Who had taken one for the team? Please not Ben or Pete ...*

Lilith watched me with a malicious twinkle in her eye. "See what they get for their efforts?" Her hands hovered over the box. She pulled them back. "No. I think it better if Jack shows you what I do to my enemies."

Dutifully, Jack stepped close and picked up the box. He froze, and his hands turned whiter. My stomach heaved, but I managed to keep the contents down as I stared at Dusty's decapitated head. His dead eyes seemed to bore into mine, and I fought the scream pulling at my throat.

Lilith actually petted Dusty's head. She ran her hand over his black hair again and again as she talked. "I'm not sure how he escaped, but he didn't get far."

Jack stepped back several steps, still holding the box. His face blanched, and he started making the gulping noise. "What … why … damn it, Lilith. He would have been more useful alive."

His eyes met mine, and the unbearable grief flitted through them. *How is he holding it together?* My eyes watered, and I blinked. A few tears fell anyway, and he snapped his attention to the floor.

"Why, Jack," Lilith purred. "Don't be upset. Your friend was deserting you."

Jack gritted his teeth and nodded. "Yes. You're right, my Queen."

She studied him. "Did he mean that much to you?"

Angrily, he stared at her in disbelief before throwing down the box and storming out. The sound of the door slamming bounced around the room.

Lilith took a step as if to go after him but stopped. She picked up the box and used it to cover Dusty's head. She took a seat on her throne.

I was left kneeling. Lilith couldn't tell me to leave, and she glared at me. "See what you've done? Now he's mad, and I'll have to deal with him pouting over his friend."

She sulked for a whole minute. "Y'know, you're becoming a thorn in my side. I should make you a vampire, too, and torture you for eternity. Then you'd never get back in Heaven … although if everything goes as planned, you won't anyway."

I wanted to jump up and beat the crap out of her. My hands shook with the need. She must have seen the fury on my face, for she smiled. "Don't worry. Tomorrow night is the New Year, and you will be reunited with your first love."

Lilith stood and smoothed her silk skirt. "I suppose I have to go coddle Jack now."

She rolled her eyes. "Men."

After taking a few steps toward the door, she paused beside me. "Don't go anywhere, Angelle. Oh, that's right. You couldn't even if you wanted to. How's it feel to be totally controlled by a man?"

She leaned close to me, and I fought the desire to jump back. "Don't tell Jack, but I will *never* let another man rule over me. After this experience, I'm sure you'll agree with me … I'll ask you then."

I so wanted to slap her. I dug my nails into the palms of my hand. Her perfume suddenly enveloped me, and I choked on its sickeningly sweet scent. She left the room, leaving me alone.

"Bitch," I mumbled.

The sound of my own voice startled me. It hadn't been loud, more like a whisper. My eyes grew wide. What did this mean? Jack hadn't released me from the no-talk clause.

The solution slapped me in the face. I should have known. My body had healed itself, making me immune to the effects of vampire blood. I was no longer a blood addict.

Holy angel wings … This was better than a souped-up Corvette on Christmas morning!

Elated, I smiled and raised my eyes to the ceiling. "Thank you, Michael. Again."

I stood and quickly went to the door, eased it open and headed for freedom. Wanting to run through the halls, I restrained myself. I clung to the shadows, grateful the candles had been blown out. Electricity would have required reflection-stealing light bulbs. I wondered how she had planned on avoiding that in the real world when she escaped this alternate reality.

I slipped past the stairs and collided with one of the *liliam*. She smacked on a piece of gum and even popped a bubble. "Where are you going?"

"On an errand for Jack."

Her face brightened. "Oh … okay."

188

What was the deal with these ditzy groupies? How had he managed to make them fall head over fangs in love with him? But then again, hadn't I been just as infatuated?

I shook my head and slipped out the front door, stopping in shock. The gray of this realm was broken by a thin layer of bright red snow. Even the falling snowflakes were red dots floating through the air.

I hurried down the steps. Time to escape. I'd have to find a way to kill Lilith later when I had help. Jack was on his evil-own.

On the bottom step, my feet suddenly refused to move. *Kate.*

I looked back at the house. There was no way I could fight all those vampires plus Jack. Somehow, he had become stronger than I was. Clearly, reinforcements were needed, and I hoped Ben and Pete weren't captured. Hopefully they were hiding in the swamp.

Stepping into the crazy-looking snow, I was amazed that the lounging gators let me. Running through the forest, I dodged tree after tree, hoping I was headed in the right direction. After a bit, I stopped to catch my breath and get my bearings.

"The itsy bitsy spider came down the water spout." The child-like voice sang only a few feet from me.

I hid behind a tree and peeked around it. One of the *liliam* sat on the ground, popping bubblegum and playing with a yo-yo.

"Down came the rain and washed the spider out."

She guarded the boat. I darted to another tree

"Out came the sun and dried up all the rain," she sang.

Three more trees, and I stood behind her. I almost felt sorry for what I was about to do.

"And the itsy bitsy spider ran up the spout again."

I stared down at her shiny black hair. Faster than lightning, my hands grabbed both of her cheeks and twisted. I hated the sound of her neck breaking, and bile rose in my throat as her body slumped back against mine.

A silver compact fell out of her hand and rolled against my foot. My mouth fell open. "Holy angel wings."

Scooping up the compact, I flipped it open and cringed at the disarray of my hair. I rolled my eyes, snapped the lid shut and shoved it in my back pocket. *Quit being such a diva.*

Obviously, Lilith didn't know one of her vain daughters had snuck in a mirror. *Yet another teenager rebelling against the rules.* At least my luck had improved thanks to her.

Looking in the direction of where the house sat, I battled the urge to go back and beat the ever living tar out of Lilith. The wiser part of me faced the boat a few yards away. I took a step toward it, but a male arm slipped around my waist. I gasped as I was yanked around and into Jack's angry embrace. Pain and anger filled his eyes.

"Let me go, Jack," I pleaded. "Or better yet, come with me."

He clenched his jaw, and he glanced toward the tree then back to me. He seemed to war with himself before he spoke. "Running is not the answer."

Grabbing my wrist, Jack pointed at the bracelet. I had less than one day to defeat Lilith. He slipped his hand into mine and led me back to the plantation.

I tried to pull away from him, but his strength surpassed mine. Fear settled in my chest. Every vampire I had ever met, including the *liliam*, was weaker than me. His superior strength baffled me, and I began to wonder if he had become something worse than a vampire. Many species bore fangs.

The large, white house appeared through the grey trees, and I patted my back pocket to assure the compact mirror was still there. Good thing, too, Lilith waited on the front porch, and her red face sent a tingle of apprehension down my spine.

"What is she doing outside, Jack?" Lilith's icy glare sent a shiver to my soul.

He slipped his hand into mine and slowed our pace to a walk. "I wanted her to see your red-winter."

The wrinkles on Lilith's forehead smoothed out as her fury subsided. Her sudden bright smile reminded me of her bubble-headed daughters. "Oh ... did she taste it?"

"Of course. Tell her what you thought of it." His voice resonated through the quietness.

"Strawberries ... it tasted like strawberries."

"Really?" Lilith raised her left eyebrow. "Tastes like blood to me."

She turned on her heel and went toward the front door but stopped and looked back at us. "Jack, bring Angelle to her room. My girls are there to start Angelle's *de-cleansing* for the ceremony. You will oversee the process in case our sacrifice becomes reticent."

"Yes, my queen," he responded and gave a slight nod of his head.

Lilith clapped her hands gleefully. "Oh, I can't wait to see the city. My girls tell me there are men for the taking on every corner."

With a swish of her skirts, she preceded us into the house. She shut herself into the library, and Jack ushered me back to my room.

What the demon wings was a de-cleansing?

***

Angelle's room in Lilith's plantation
Alternate Reality
Sunday, December 31ˢᵗ, 5:30 PM
Countdown: 0 Days 22 Hours 29 Minutes 59 Seconds

I woke, not realizing I had fallen asleep on the couch. The room was empty, and I pulled my memories together through the cobwebs of sleep.

When Jack had brought me back to my room, there had been a tray of cookies and two plastic cups of hot tea on the coffee table. His groupies had been with us, so when he told me to drink up, I had to do as he bade in order to keep up the illusion that I was still under his command. I didn't want to, and the bitterness in the tea confirmed there was something else besides sugar in the liquid. Within minutes, a warm drowsiness had swept over me, and the last thing I remembered was curling up on the couch.

Yawning, I shook the stiffness out of my limbs. I looked at the bracelet ticking down to the riddle's deadline. *Less than a day to defeat her royal loveliness.*

I felt my back pocket, relaxing when my fingers touched the compact mirror. Jack had left it.

Keys rattled at the bedroom door, and a few seconds later, he peeked in. "Hi."

I glared at him. Clearly he didn't expect me to be cordial after sending me into a drug induced sleep.

He pushed open the door and entered, followed by two of his groupies. He knelt in front of me and stared intently into my eyes. "I hope you feel well rested. You'll need all your strength for tonight's ceremony."

Truth be told, I did. Energy coursed through me, and I was ready to give Lilith a good fight.

"The tea had a restorative, cleansing herb in it … *eleuthero,* also known as Siberian ginseng," he admitted. "Unfortunately, the stuff also causes drowsiness, but Lilith expected that. Even I took a nap."

I frowned, feeling stubborn. He wasn't getting off the hook so easily.

Jack slipped his hand into mine and stood, pulling me up with him. "It's time to get you ready for the ceremony. Remember, not a peep out of your mouth until you're told to."

He winked at me before handing me over to the nearest groupie. Leaving him behind, they led me out of the bedroom and down a series of hallways and stairways until we ended up in the lowest section of the house. One of the *liliam* opened the door.

A giant floor of stinky swamp mud encompassed the center of the room, and we stepped onto a wooden boardwalk that lined the edges. Blue candles lit the area. Turquoise gems lay scattered about the boardwalk, and ocean-scented incense filled the air.

The *liliam* led me to the other side, where steps went down into the mud. The most assertive of the women took charge. "Strip down and get in."

When I hesitated, she crossed her arms and said, "I am so ready to get out of this realm for good, I have no qualms about ripping the clothes off and pushing you in."

Let the bitch try. Jack had told me not to talk. He hadn't said anything about obeying. I crossed my arms and stared at them with a smile.

She reached out to grab my arm. I sidestepped, grabbed hers and shoved her into the mud pool. The other two *liliam* attacked me at once, and they ended up in the same predicament. I headed for the door, but when I opened it, Jack blocked my path.

"What part of playing along do you not get?" he whispered. "I knew you'd have trouble with this."

I shrugged. He stepped toward me, towering over me. I backed up to the edge of the boardwalk.

"Would you like me to undress you?" he asked, his voice louder.

Hesitating, the lust demon on my back sent an image of Jack pulling my shirt off me. *Yes,* I thought. *Why, yes I would.*

I shook my head, and while I could have fought him, I had to keep up the pretense that I was under his spell. The *liliam* watched me closely.

"No. I can manage," I replied as meekly as possible.

He glared at me, backed out of the room and closed the door. I slowly faced the three *liliam*. They had climbed out of the mud pool and stood glaring at me. Begrudgingly, I went back over to the pool steps, stripped down, and walked into the mud bath.

One of the women got in with me and showed me where there were ledges to sit on. "We do this a lot, but this time is special. You have to be calm for the ceremony. So relax."

Ha. Fat chance.

However, I did as they asked and attempted to relax. A light music filled the room, and all three of the *liliam* began chanting. "May thy troubles fade away, and the beast be held at bay."

They continued chanting as one of them dipped a cup in the mud and poured it over my head, massaging the smelly gook into my hair. I tried not to gag.

This is supposed to help me relax?

Amazingly, I eventually adjusted to the smell. The music, the soft chanting and the incense began to seep into my being, and a calm state of mind settled over me. The energy remained just below the surface, but I felt oddly at peace. The spell was working, and I suddenly didn't care that I was about to become Nate's plaything again.

The inner voice in the back of my head cared, because she was screaming and cursing. Her words became muffled as a fog seemed to settle over my brain. I knew I should be frightened but the spa treatment seemed to be working.

I lost track of the time, but eventually, the *liliam* led me out of the pool. Mud dripped down my back and squished between my toes. They made me lay down on the boardwalk. They continued chanting, keeping up the room's calm ambiance.

Thirty minutes later, the *liliam* had cleaned up and turned their attention back to me. Most of the mud on my body had dried and pinched my skin uncomfortably.

Attached to the wall was a metal arm with five shower heads hooked to it. The *liliam* positioned it above me and blasted me with lukewarm water. They handed me a sudsy bath sponge, a bottle of shampoo and conditioner and let me clean up.

Once I was done, they helped me into a plush red bathrobe and covered my head with the hood. Leading me to the door, one of the *liliam* handed my clothes to Jack.

"She's ready," said the one who had helped me in the mud pool. She smiled sweetly at me.

Feeling as if I were on cloud nine, I smiled goofily back at her.

What the demon-wings was wrong with me? I should be wanting to kick her ass not wanting to give her a sisterly hug.

Jack led me to another room and left me alone with more of Lilith's daughters. They painted my finger and toenails a bright red. They also painted a huge red pentagram on my chest, right beside my tattoo. I wasn't happy about that one bit, but the calming spell soon made me forget the diagram was even there.

Once they put makeup on my face and fixed my hair, they helped me into a bright red wedding dress. They fussed over me to get everything just right, then threw open the door and let in Jack.

His mouth dropped.

Where's a mirror when you need one?

The dress pushed my boobs up and together, revealing the tip of my cross tattoo with the cat in the center of it. The red pentagram was clearly visible on my chest, and I wished I could scrub it off.

Jack whistled and held out a bouquet filled with red and black roses. "I made this for you. A bride needs flowers, whether she's willing or not."

Taking the bouquet, I noticed the roses were tied to a thick stick that was as long as my arm. I quirked an eyebrow at him, and he simply smiled. "Something old. I found it while picking the roses from Lilith's garden."

He held out his arm, and I slipped my right hand into the crook. Time to face the devil.

***

CHAPTER 20

Lilith's Plantation
Alternate Reality
Sunday, December 31ˢᵗ, 11:30 PM
Countdown: 0 Days 16 Hours 29 Minutes 59 Seconds

*Just concentrate on taking one step in front of the
other.*

Jack took his time ushering me through the hallways.
My heart fluttered like a mouse being chased by a hawk.
Nate's face flashed in my head.

As a young angel, he'd been handsome and full of
promise. Years later, his elegant face became twisted
with hate and jealousy. The devilish eyebrows were the
most obvious change, but his eyes had changed from a
rich, almond-brown to a tar-black. He often used tar to
torment his captured souls.

Tar … I shuddered. At first, I had been his guinea pig.
Memories of tortures long gone caused my steps to
falter. My knees buckled, and my weight fell on Jack's
arm. He stopped briefly until I had regained my
composure.

We started forward again and passed the doors
leading to Lilith's throne room. We traveled through a
few more halls before he led me up a set of stairs and
entered the attic. Boxes lined the pathway, and in one
section, furniture lay unused beneath dusty drop cloths.

Jack stopped before a door. He hesitated before
crushing me to him in a desperate hug. His lips hovered

over mine, and the attic suddenly seemed stifling hot as my body reacted to his nearness. His eyes were filled with despair, and my heart lurched.

His soft lips brushed mine, and I melted against him. If I'd been chocolate, he'd have been a gooey mess. I closed my eyes, savoring the sweet sensation of his mouth. His tongue pushed between my lips and tangled with mine. The pleasure of it rolled through me, pushing aside all thoughts for just a moment.

Nate.

My insides grew cold. I could have sworn even Jack felt my heart ice over, for he stopped kissing me and turned around to open the door. The roof lay shrouded in darkness. My eyes quickly adjusted, and apparently, so did Jack's.

Row upon row of chairs lined up to view the so-called wedding ceremony. The *liliam* filled the chairs, but not all of Lilith's daughters were present. There were too many of them to fit on the roof.

Ben and Pete sat in the first row, both catatonic. My heart jumped in my throat. How had she caught them?

Lilith awaited us at the altar, which held unlit candles and various dark gems and objects. There was also food that I recognized as some of Nate's favorites – cake, spaghetti and wine. She had lain it out as a way to invite him in to this realm. *Smart bitch.*

The groom was missing, and for that, I was grateful. Kate stood as my maid of honor, but she stared into space as if in a trance. I trembled and held tightly to Jack's arm. He gave no indication that he noticed, and he walked me right up to Lilith.

In the empty groom's space was a containment triangle. Three black onyx were connected by a white chalk line to form a triangle. Also placed around the outside of the triangle were unlit candles and gems representing the four elements: Earth (gemstones), Air (incense), Fire (candlelight) and Water (fresh flowers).

Jack moved me into the triangle. He let go and stepped back

"Who gives this woman away today?" Lilith giggled. "Oh, right. That would be me."

Her beauty shone as if she were the bride. The customary lily sat in the middle of her crown. Her lilac colored gown clung to her ample bosom and voluptuous hips.

Lilith slapped her hands together. "Well … how can we have a wedding without a groom?"

My mouth instantly felt dry. *Too bad. Let's go home.*

Kneeling in front of the altar, she bowed her head and raised her hands. "Dear old friend, we welcome you to cross. Step into our world. We'll gladly pay the cost."

After taking a sip of the wine, she took a bite from the meal and the dessert. She mumbled the words again, rose regally to her feet and faced us.

"Jack," Lilith purred with her eyes on my face. "Tell her to call for Nate."

He hesitated before begrudgingly giving me the order. Biting my tongue, I tried to stall. I looked from Lilith to Jack and back to her again, but I was tired of playing the puppet. It was time for a bit of rebellion.

In one swift motion, I pulled the stake free of the bouquet, tossing aside the flowers as I did. It was easier than I thought to plunge the stake right where Lilith's heart should have been. And yes, I said should have been. For Lilith didn't crumple into dust before my eyes. She merely stared at me with hate and refused to die.

"Look what you have done to my dress!"

The second I realized Lilith wasn't dead or even in some kind of coma, two things happened at once. I shook the mirror out of my sleeve and into my left palm. At the same time, an unseen hand pulled the stake out of Lilith and slammed the stake into Jack's chest. My mouth fell open, and my own heart seemed to explode in pain as I waited for his dusty remains to settle over me.

Fortunately, that didn't happen.

Jack's face froze in shock as he dropped to his knees. His eyes rolled back in his head as his body slumped unconscious to the floor. My knees buckled.

Dancing demon-wings, Lilith must have turned him.

Hands grasped my arms from behind. I looked at them, expecting to see feminine fingers. Instead, they were huge, demonic hands and fire-engine red. The fingernails were filed to a point, and their tips drew dots of blood where they dug into my flesh.

Lilith suddenly stood before me, and her fingers slid around my throat. "Did you think it would be that easy?" Her eyes were completely red. "How do you think I've stayed alive all these years?"

I kept the mirror hidden in my palm as the demon held me still. I glanced over my shoulder to see he had a fire-engine red body that stood seven foot tall, and I had to look up to see his face. He had jet black hair and curling horns protruded from his head.

My gaze focused back to Lilith as her fingers slipped away from my throat.

Her sickly-sweet smile made me nauseated. "You're no longer Jack's slave."

I shrugged. "So sue me."

"Call for Nate."

"Yeah, right."

Lilith's hand shot out, and her fingers dug into my cheeks. "Call him … NOW!"

Locking eyes with the she-bitch, I saw the crazy in the depths of hers. Guess being locked up for over a hundred years would do that to a being. I talked through fish-puckered lips. "Fine, but only if you let me go first."

She laughed. "Yeah, right. Call Nate now, or I'll make sure Jack stays dead."

A shadow fell over my heart. Jack had become the innocent who needed saving. If it meant sacrificing myself … "I will go to Nate willingly, but only if you let

Jack and Kate go. And I need proof, or you can go screw yourself."

Lilith let go of my face and waved her hand. Jack and Kate vanished, and I had to admit I was taken aback. Lilith had this much power? Would she continue to have it in the real world?

I couldn't let that happen.

"Happy now?" she asked.

My eyes narrowed. "That doesn't mean they are back in the real world."

She rolled her eyes, swirled her left hand in the air and created a bubble. Kate knelt over Jack as he lay on the porch of my house. Just as instantly, the bubble vanished.

"Call him," she ordered.

I really did not want to see my ex, but she had upheld her end of the bargain. I took a deep breath and glanced at Lilith. "Isn't there another way you can get out of this realm?"

"I can just as easily bring your friends back," Lilith growled.

"Really? Because I had to use an owl key …" I replied.

She began circling her hand and pulling a spell together. I held up my hands. "Ok. Fine. But don't say I didn't warn you. Nate is famous for twisting your deepest desires on you."

When I had first become human and began running the bar, I came up with the fishbowl idea. It worked like a charm. I'd collect the business cards, and Jeneen would help me find lost souls to save.

One day I pulled a card that only had one sentence on it. I read it out loud and inadvertently called upon my ex. When I had pulled the card, I hadn't realized there was a spell attached to those words, one that activated only with my voice when I read it out loud.

I now said the words I'd only made the mistake of saying once before. "For a good time, call Nate."

***

Swamp
Alternate Reality
Monday, January 1st, 12:00 AM
Countdown: 0 Days 15 Hours 59 Minutes 59 Seconds

Lilith laughed, and it sounded like a child's. "What a devil he is."

Beside her, the air began to turn to static dots. After a few seconds, they merged into the shape of a man – Nate. He wore a black and white tuxedo, and his hair was slicked back.

The second his form was solid, Lilith said, "Nate, I bind thee from causing harm to those in this realm. I bind thee to the triangle. I bind thee, Nate, to the triangle in which you stand."

He held his hands up, wiggled his fingers and laughed. "Okay, we get it, Lilith. I am *bound*."

She smiled coquettishly and waved a polished fingernail at him. "You fooled me once. You won't do it again."

Nate gave her a slight bow before pivoting on his heel to face me. He looked me over from head to toe and back again. Letting out a low whistle, he crossed his arms.

"Well well well," he drawled. "Angelle."

"Hello, Nate," I replied.

"You look ravishing." Nate turned to Lilith. "As do you."

Ever the gentleman, Nate's oily slickness showed through the polite niceties. Below the handsome surface lay a deadly snake ready to strike and pull one into Hell's arms. I wanted to step back from him but was still held fast by the demon behind me.

"Why, thank you," Lilith responded.

"So you managed to get her here of her own free will."

"Yes, my lord," she said. "I used her friends as bait."

Nate's black eyes stared into mine, and my flesh crawled. Apparently, they had been negotiating this deal for quite a while.

"Why go to this extreme, Nate?" I asked. "All you had to do was make sure I didn't solve the riddle."

Letting go of Lilith, he stepped between her and myself. With his back to her, he held a finger to his lips, and his black eyes twinkled. I narrowed my eyes, wondering who was getting played by the devil – Lilith or me.

Grabbing my right hand, Nate stepped beside me. The demon let go of me and knelt behind us. Without a second's hesitation, I popped open the compact in my left hand and whipped it up in front of me.

Lilith froze, and her eyes widened as she stared into the little mirror. Her mouth fell open, and her scream would have shattered a normal human's ears. I watched in morbid, horrified fascination as the mirror pulled her flesh off her bones and into the mirror. The creature left standing before me was a small, horrid old hag, and she still screeched.

I looked at Nate, who stared gleefully at Lilith's true form. My stomach twisted, and I became anxious to get rid of the fallen angel.

"In Jesus' name, get thee, Satan, from my sight," I cried out, and Nate's form sizzled and smoke rose from his body.

"Aw, come on, Angie," he whined.

"I hate that nickname," I spat just as he went up in a puff of smoke. I swiveled around and face the red demon. Around his neck hung a black onyx that kept him safe from mirrors. I grabbed the stone, yanked it from the chain and pointed the compact at him.

A Sangre demon ...

The mirror pulled him into it. I snapped the compact shut and tucked it into the bodice of my dress. Turning on my heel, I was ready to get the demon-wings out of this place.

My ears hurt from the screeching around me. I looked at the rows and rows of *liliam*, who were now as hideous and haggy as their mother. The humans amongst them stood out and were now much more appealing than their captors.

Wrinkly, cold fingers slid around my wrist. The hag version of Lilith had made it to my side, and she tried to reach for the compact. I easily held her at bay. "Seriously, Lilith?"

I pushed her away. Though it was gentle, she stumbled back, lost her balance and fell on her butt. I lifted my left eyebrow as she struggled to get up. It was sad and pathetic.

She tried to send you back to Hell.

That single thought launched me into action. I looked at Lilith. She held her hands up and shook her head as I approached.

"No. Please." Her faint voice crackled with oldness.

My mercy had fled. It was time to send this manipulative loser to Hell.

I knelt over her, holding her down with one hand. A tear slid down her gray, wrinkled cheek, but I refused to let it affect me. Her cracked lips moved. "Would you kill your grandmother?"

"If I had a grandmother like you," I punched her in the mouth. "Sure."

Lilith's fangs crumbled upon impact of my fist. She screeched as her body jerked at odd angles. A few seconds later, she quit squirming, and death filled her eyes. Her body exploded in dust, and silence pressed eerily upon me. Since I had taken Lilith's powers away from her with the mirror, I knew she wasn't a vampire but a Sangre demon.

"Next time, wear that black onyx necklace," I spat. Standing, I kicked at her ashes. "Of course, that didn't help your Sangre demon lover."

I faced the wedding guests. All the *liliam* were staring at me with open mouths. The second I took a step toward them, they scrambled to their feet, intent on escaping.

Fate had other plans for them. One by one, their bodies spasmed like their mother's had, popping into tiny bits of dust that drifted like cotton seed on a windy day. Eventually, all Lilith's daughters became vampire dust that covered all the chairs and few humans.

Jack ...

My heart constricted painfully, and tears filled my eyes. Did he explode into dust as well? I had no way to contact Kate as my cell phone had been taken from me, and I had no idea if it would work in this realm anyway. Urgency to get back filled my soul.

The bracelet flared with warmth, and the gold it was made of emanated a brilliant light. Tiny fireworks sparked from the words, erasing them from the gold and eating up the bracelet until it disappeared.

"Show off," I mumbled, picturing Robert as he called the bracelet back into his realm.

Relief should have flooded through me and lifted the weight off my shoulders. Riddle solved. Bad girl vanquished. Innocents saved. Go me.

But the idea of Jack exploding into dust put a huge damper on my victory.

***

Scorned

CHAPTER 21

Lilith's Plantation
Alternate Reality
Monday, January 1ˢᵗ, 12:30 AM

With the demise of Lilith, the realm she had been trapped in began to come apart. Almost instantaneously, the plantation's beauty faded to a broken down wreck. Moss covered the roof and crunched beneath my feet.

The moon broke free from the clouds and lit up the plantation and swamp. Ben and Pete stood, looking around in confusion. The five humans did the same.

Kicking off the high heeled shoes, I rushed to Ben and Pete. "We have to get out of here before this roof caves in."

I swiped at my tear-stained face, pushing back more tears. At the moment, there was no way to know if Jack had perished with Lilith and her daughters. *Think positive, girl.*

"What's wrong?" Ben asked.

Taking a deep breath, I voiced my fears about Jack. Sadly, saying it out loud made it seem even more plausible. Depression parked its big butt on my chest, making it difficult to breathe.

For once, Ben remained speechless. Pete pulled me into a hug, and whispered, "Let go, let God."

Pete was right. If Jack had disappeared out of my life (literally and figuratively), we just weren't meant to be together. I had to take a leap of faith, and trust in God's plans for me. Easier said than done.

Numbed, I helped Ben and Pete with the humans. I led the way across the rooftop, kicking at the bulky skirt of my dress, which had become heavy and cumbersome. As we entered the attic, I paused to tear off the bottom part of the dress before following the pathway. Nothing jumped out to get us, though I was ready with the stake if that happened.

Once we got to the other side of the attic, I noticed that the door hung on one hinge, as if someone had kicked it in. The floors beneath my feet suddenly shook as the plantation's boards creaked and moaned. The humans behind me screamed and fell to their knees. The mini-earthquake lasted only seconds, but it pushed our nerves closer to the edge of losing control.

"Come on," I said and pushed the door open as much as possible.

Disappointment flooded through me. The steps had disintegrated into a pile of wood ten feet below. The attic rafters groaned and shifted, and the floor beneath our feet began to crack.

Ben jumped down, dancing upon the wood until it settled beneath his feet. Then he held his hands up. Without a word, Pete and I helped the five humans over the side and into Ben's waiting arms. Once done, Pete easily dropped beside Ben.

In normal clothing, a jump like that would be nothing for me. The dress I had on made it a bit more difficult, but I took the plunge. The material actually cushioned my awkward landing.

Ben helped me up and led me out of the rubble into the hallway. The building shook in another mini-quake, and we ran down the hallway with Pete in the lead. I took up the rear.

When we passed Lilith's throne room, something made me stop. The others rushed ahead, and I let them go without me. Call me materialistic, but I wanted my things back.

I knew it was a long shot that they would be in her throne room, but I recalled the china cabinet filled with items from Lilith's conquests. Racing around the room, I stepped over holes that appeared in the floor as I broke open the doors of every cabinet. Of course, the items I sought were in the last cabinet, the one closest to the throne.

Grabbing my cell phone, I tried to make a call to Chadwick, but the battery was dead.

Figures.

The plantation floor shook, more violently this time, and the middle of the room screamed as it cracked into a huge gaping hole. Ben appeared in the doorway.

"What the hell are you doing?" he yelled at me.

I scooped up my Walther PPK and held it up. "Getting what's mine."

"Well, hurry up, unless you want to remain a part of Lilith's home."

Next to my things were items I knew belonged to Jack and the others. I grabbed everything, including Kate and Jack's cell phones before carefully making my way around the hole-filled floor. Ben took some of the stuff from me, and we ran through the crumbling plantation.

We caught up to Pete and the humans on the plantation's front porch, freezing at the sight of so many alligators covering the front yard.

"I got this," Pete said, shifting his hand into Werewolf mode. A low growl emanated from him, and the gators raised their heads.

The largest one - the one with the white tufts of hair – rose on its hind legs. Bob the Were-gator shifted into complete and naked human-form. For an old guy, he had a well-defined body.

Pete took a fighting stance, and the rest of us did the same. Bob held his hands up with his fingers splayed in a non-threatening gesture. "No need fer all that now, son."

Pete's stance relaxed, but I could tell by his tense shoulders that he was ready for anything. "Why you playing nice now?"

Bob pointed at the plantation. "No longer under that she-devil's spell."

He looked at me, and said, "Thank you for that, ma'am. She had all the gator-men bespelled to do her bidding."

I shrugged. "No problem."

Bob turned to the Were-gators. "Let's go, boys. Our women will be mighty glad to see us."

With a wink and a growl, he shifted back into gator-form and led his clan into the swamp.

We hurried to the boat, and luckily, it was big enough to fit eight people. Ben drove us back to the cypress tree, but it was no longer the huge, prehistoric tree. The good news was that the monster gator was gone. The bad news was that our portal had disappeared.

"I know where we are now," Pete said. "I fish this area all the time. Well, not in this dimension, but ..."

He took over driving the boat, but as it was still dark, he had to go through the swamp at a maddeningly slow speed. The dark water slid by, and enormous trees loomed up out of nowhere.

When we finally made it back to dry land, the sun peeped over the horizon. Ben tied the boat to an old rickety dock, and Pete helped everyone out. The dress hindered my movements, but with their assistance, I soon stood on solid ground.

Across the street was a gas station/convenience store that looked like it had been there since the early 1900's. I pushed open the glass door, and my red dress caught in the metal frame. Yanking the material free, the nail ripped a hole in the taffeta. Uncaring, I paused and made a quick survey of the store. The clock on the wall confirmed that it was about 6:30 am.

The only person inside was an employee. The Cajun lady tending the register stared at me with her mouth open. Apparently, they didn't get many fancily dressed customers.

"Do you have a phone I can use?" I asked.

"Not for customer use," she said in a clipped tone.

Frustrated, I swirled around to Ben, and asked, "I don't suppose you have any money …"

He pulled out his wallet, which I had recovered from Lilith's cabinet of conquests. There was a stash of ten dollar bills, and he handed me two.

Turning to the lady, I waved them in the air. "Will twenty bucks change your mind?"

She pulled an old black rotary phone from beneath the counter and set it next to the register. I handed her the money and called Chadwick, head of The Human Society. After I explained our situation, he agreed to send a few vehicles to pick us up. One would be to take the humans back to headquarters where they would get help on processing what had just happened and then be reunited with their families. Another vehicle would be for me, Ben and Pete.

"Please have them hurry, Chadwick," I said. After telling him where we were, I hung up the phone and pushed it toward the lady. "Thank you."

Ben quickly paid for a handful of chips, cookies, candy and drinks. He headed for the door, and I followed him back to the boat where Pete kept watch over the humans.

"Well?" he asked.

"The cavalry is on the way," Ben said, passing out the food and drink.

The dock rocked under my feet as I contemplated where to sit. The dress made everything difficult, so I pointed at the gas station where there were some chairs. "I'll wait over there."

Trudging back across the street, I plopped into a white chair. My dress cushioned behind against the hard plastic. Waiting was definitely the hardest part. Fear for Jack consumed my brain, and I bent my head, relying on the only thing that would help me through worrying over Jack – praying.

***

Angelle's House
Watson, La
Monday, January 1st, 10 AM

Pete pulled the big SUV into my driveway and rolled slowly up to the house. The vehicle rocked to a stop, and I flung open the door, jumped out and raced inside. Fear stole my breath and made my mouth dry.

I threw open the front door. "Kate?"

"In here," she called from the guest bedroom.

I wanted to run to her, but suddenly my feet felt like lead. Terror had done that too. Taking a deep breath, I shook the feeling away and approached the room like a woman facing her fate.

Please don't let Jack be dust.

I chewed on the inside of my lip. The door to the bedroom remained partially open, and placing my hand against the cold wood, I pushed the door all the way.

Please.

Kate sat in a chair placed next to the bed. Her disheveled hair and haunted eyes stood testimony to her own night from Hell. Blood covered her clothes and cheeks, and her arm rested on the equally blood-drenched bed.

"I did what I could," she whispered.

Jack lay on top of the ruined bedspread. My knees wobbled as relief chased back the apprehension. I placed a hand on my heart, closed my eyes and whispered, "Thank you, Lord."

"He's not out of the woods yet," Kate said.

My eyes opened, and I immediately stepped closer to the bed. The stake lay beside him, and blood soaked towels covered his bare abdomen. His white dress shirt had been ripped open.

"The stake missed his heart, but he's lost a lot of blood. I didn't know if I should call an ambulance or not," she said.

Gingerly removing the towels, my mouth set in a firm line. The wound had healed. My fingers traced the scar that faded beneath my touch.

"Glad you didn't. He's no longer human," I stated dully.

His chest rose and fell steadily. Kate slipped her arm around my waist and pulled me against her side in a half hug.

"He'll be okay then. He'll pull through," she assured me.

"Maybe for the time being, but in the long haul, his soul's in danger."

"Did Lilith make him a vampire?" Kate whispered.

I shook my head. "I've been mulling everything over and over, and while he acts like a vampire, he's not. If she had made him one, he would have exploded in a world of dust like all the rest. No, he's not a vampire, but something much worse – a Sangre demon."

The red wedding dress suddenly felt heavy. "I need to get this off."

I stepped away from her and Jack. "Guess I better go get cleaned up. I probably smell like something that crawled out of the swamp, too."

"Well, maybe a little ..." Kate smiled as she sat in a chair across the room. "I'll keep an eye on him for you."

"Thanks." I pulled the door until it closed with a soft thud and went to the bathroom in my bedroom.

I locked myself in and pulled the compact mirror from my bodice. Reaching for the light switch, my fingers paused as I contemplated smashing the mirror with a brick. Ultimately, I knew I couldn't do that as I had no idea if destroying the Sangre demon trapped inside the mirror would destroy Jack as well.

I flipped the switch down.

"Robert."

The temperature dropped, and the hackles on my neck rose.

A soft whistle of appreciation echoed in the bathroom. "Nice dress. The last time I saw you in a dress--"

I held up my hand. "Don't remind me."

I held out the mirror. "Can you keep this in a safe place?"

"What is it?"

"It holds a Sangre demon and Lilith's beauty."

His cold fingers closed around my hand. "I know of just the spot."

"Thank you," I whispered. Silence reigned between us.

"What's wrong?" Robert asked.

My voice faltered. "I still can't get over the fact that Jack tried to make me a blood addict. Regardless of why he did it, he still did it. He knew I'd be forever bound to a vampire ... er, demon."

Anger welled up inside of me, and anxiety clenched in my chest. My heart struggled to get past the feeling. I felt something for Jack, but did I trust him?

Robert's cool hand patted my own. "He knew you'd heal."

I nodded. "I guess."

The room started to warm up, and I felt him begin to fade away. "I've gotta go. The boss man is calling."

I nodded. "See ya."

Plodding back to the bedroom, I placed around Jack's neck the black onyx that I had taken from the Sangre

214

Demon. I had no idea how long it would take for him to heal but hoped the natural stone would help. Kate helped me clean up the bed, removing and replacing the blood soaked cover and sheets. Once done, she went to my room to take a nap while Ben and Pete went home.

Resting my arms on the bed, my weary eyes closed. I hadn't realized I had fallen asleep until Kate gently shook my shoulder. Groggy, I looked at Jack, but he still slept.

"I made you some dinner," she said. "Come eat."

Nodding, I straightened the covers over Jack before following her to the kitchen. Ben and Pete sat at the table, cleaned up and presentable.

"Hey," I mumbled and took a seat. We fell into silence as we ate. Forks tinged against plates, and glasses clanked against the table. Everyone was weary from the battle – physically and mentally.

Once done, we left the dishes for later and slipped into the living room to watch mindless television.

Jack suddenly appeared in the doorway. He wore only his briefs, and his half-naked body momentarily blindsided me. So I didn't anticipate his next move until I was on the floor with his teeth hovering inches over my neck.

Technically, I was the only human in the room. So it made sense he attacked me. I could tell by the red film over his eyes he wasn't himself. Fortunately, my other vampire friends were themselves. They grabbed him and hauled his ass off me. Apparently, he was weak from lack of food.

"He needs blood," I croaked as I struggled to get off the floor. My hands and legs shook as I watched the demon in Jack fight for control. It took one old vampire, one Werewolf and one weredog to keep him from attacking me. He was pretty strong for one so young.

"There's blood bags in the fridge," I yelled.

215

As they took care of feeding Jack's new-found thirst, I rushed to the bathroom and inspected my throat in the mirror. *No holes* ... So I was good to go, but try telling that to my human nerves. While this body was incredibly strong, it was nothing compared to what the angelic body I once had so long ago and had impulsively tossed away.

Jack appeared in the doorway, and I froze. Part of me feared he'd attack me again.

He shifted his stance and looked around uncomfortably. "Um, hey."

My heart flip-flopped at the haunted look on his face. He stepped closer to me and placed his hands on my shoulders. Our eyes locked in the mirror, and my anger at being made a blood addict melted, especially my heart. Perhaps I *was* still addicted to him.

Jack pulled me back against him, and I closed my eyes. The heat of his body momentarily obliterated any thought, and I wanted to remain frozen in time. My hope for that shattered when he spoke.

"We need to talk."

I kept my eyes closed. "Do we have to?"

"You know better."

I looked at his reflection and sighed. "Okay."

He turned me around, and at first, I thought he intended to kiss me. He pulled me into a hug. Gee, if I was so angry with him, why was I letting him so near to me? Was I really as mad as I had been?

Jack stepped back, took my hand and led me into my bedroom. He shut and locked the door, indicating for me to sit in the chair. He sat on the edge of the bed and ran his hands through his hair. "I'm sorry for trying to send you back to Hell."

I crossed my arms and sat back in the chair. I flung one leg over the other and swung it in agitation. "Well? Is that all your sorry for?"

His baby blues narrowed. "Isn't that why you're so mad?"

I closed my eyes. Men. "So was it your idea to make me a blood addict, or was it Lilith's?"

He had the decency to look ashamed. "Well ..."

My fingernails dug into my forearms as I refrained from jumping up and slapping him. "Why?"

"I couldn't think of a better way of convincing her that I was on her side."

"Why didn't you try to kill her?"

He crossed his arms. "I tried that. Didn't work. So I thought you'd know how to kill her, but the only way to get you there was through her ... which meant acting like I was on her side. Besides, I knew you'd heal."

"How'd you end up there in the first place?"

Jack gulped. "When Trina bit the inside of my lip, I knew I was in trouble. She immediately had control over me and ..." He hung his head, unable to look at me. "Part of me liked it - for a while, anyway, until she started grilling me about you. I wanted to lie. Hell, I *tried* to lie, but it made me physically ill."

I could see the disgust for his actions on his face.

"The last night as a free man was the night when you woke from being staked by the crazy blood addict." Anger flashed across his face like a shooting star. He shook his head, jumped to his feet and started pacing. "Something dark had entered my soul. I'm ashamed to admit it, but I couldn't think of anything but Trina."

"Gee," I mumbled. "Thanks. What a way to keep a girl's confidence up."

"No, not like that. Not like I think of you all the time." He hurried to explain. He stood and crossed his arms. "Man, this is hard to explain."

More stoic silence.

"The darkness in my soul ..." He re-took his position on the edge of the bed and looked me in the eye. "The dark side we all have."

I nodded and swallowed over a lump. "Nate planted it in humans. The day Eve ate the apple. Darkness was born from that tainted fruit."

Jack pointed at me. "Right. So you see, it was that darkness which answered the siren's call."

"So your mood swings …"

"Were the darkness … I am constantly fighting for control." He still refused to look up from the floor. "I followed Trina and went willingly to my jail, so to speak. The night I saw you hanging from the tree … It was like the sight of you reminded me I needed to embrace the good and fight the dark."

Oh, nicely put. My chest swelled unexpectedly with love. *Stupid heart.*

Jack slid off the bed and knelt in front of me. "I'm sorry for making you a blood addict, but in my defense, I knew you would heal. By the time you arrived to save me, I'd already been bitten by the Sangre demon two times. I was under his control, and as he was her mate, Lilith manipulated him. I did what I could to help you."

"Well, you did a fantastic job, and the award goes to …"

"Angelle, please! There was no way to communicate with you. Lilith can hear ten miles away, so she would have picked up even the tiniest of whispers. She even heard you, Ben and Pete stumbling around in the woods."

I nibbled the inside of my lip. She had better hearing than I did. *Wow, impressive.*

"I'm sorry." His face twisted in pain.

"Yeah, I've heard that before," I snorted.

"And I'll keep saying it until you accept it."

My heart fluttered at the mere thought of what I was about to tell him. "I'm not talking about hearing it from you before. The way you say it reminds me of how Nate used to apologize after beating me."

218

Jack's mouth fell open a little. "I … I don't beat women. Please don't compare me to him."

He was right. Nobody should be compared to the devil.

"We need to take this slow," I whispered.

"I promise to treat you right," he said.

"We're eternal," My lips trembled. "You're now a demon. I'm an ex-angel. It's going to take a long time, and a lot of work between you and me."

Jack took my face in both his hands. "I'm willing if you are."

He slowly lowered his head until his lips touched mine. I sank into his kiss, letting him work his wicked magic on my mouth.

Midnight chose that moment to make her presence known. She jumped on the bed and forced her huge body between us.

Wait, huge?

I pulled back from Jack to stare at the kitten I had saved from Hell only eleven days ago. The black cat purred and rubbed her head lovingly against my arm. Then she shook her body, and wings sprouted from her back. She shape shifted into a tiny Pegasus. I had saved Medusa's pet. Fabulous!

The End

ACKNOWLEDGEMENTS

Nancy S. Brandt – thank you for helping me see the true path this book was supposed to be on. You are a fabulous editor and writer. Hugs!

For those who continue to support me: My parents (Frank & Betty Ault), my in-laws (Charles & Gail), my sons (Mike & Chris), my many brothers and sisters (including in-laws), and to my HeartLa friends.

The Rowdy Girls – Nancy and Meredith … good memories, good times, good friends. Rowdy on!

Steven R. Brandt and Samantha Summers – Thank you for helping polish up this version!

ABOUT THE AUTHOR

Josephine Templeton represents angels, demons, vampires, romance and sometimes humans. She is an urban fantasy novelist, a member of HeartLa (the Baton Rouge chapter of Romance Writers of America) and a freelance writer. She has several published novels under her wings (from historical romance to vampire romance).

Her Social Media:
www.josephinetempleton.com
Good Reads (www.goodreads.com)
FaceBook https://m.facebook.com/josephine.templeton
Twitter – https://twitter.com/theladyjojo

Made in the USA
Columbia, SC
22 February 2026

79705353R00128